Squishy Taylor

and the First Three Adventures

hardie grant EGMONT

Squishy Taylor and the First Three Adventures
published in 2017 by
Hardie Grant Egmont
Ground Floor, Building 1, 658 Church Street
Richmond, Victoria 3121, Australia
www.hardiegrantegmont.com.au

A CiP record for this title is available from the
National Library of Australia.

Text copyright © 2017 Ailsa Wild
Illustrations copyright © 2017 Ben Wood
Series design copyright © 2017 Hardie Grant Egmont

Series design by Stephanie Spartels
Illustrations by Ben Wood
Typeset by Cannon Typesetting

Printed in Australia by McPherson's Printing Group, Maryborough,
Victoria, an accredited ISO AS/NZS 14001 Environmental
Management System printer.

1 3 5 7 9 10 8 6 4 2

The paper in this book is FSC® certified.
FSC® promotes environmentally responsible,
socially beneficial and economically viable
management of the world's forests.

Contents

For Toby and Emily and
their wild bonus family.

– Ailsa

For Jess, my new bonus sister.

– Ben

and the Bonus Sisters

Chapter One

Baby is on the change mat, pooey and kicking. Dad looks flustered. 'Please, Squishy,' he asks me, 'can you get the baby wipes? They're in the car.'

Squishy Taylor to the rescue.

I spin and grab the car key, ducking out our front door to pause in the hallway. Lift or stairs? **Which is more fun?** Stairs, of course – all eleven flights of them. I bolt past the other apartments to the stairwell, then leap down the steps like a **ninja-gazelle**.

I slow
down at the
bottom before
I get to the car
park. It's always
been a bit dark and creepy down here.

Our car is right at the far end, with the other cars from the eleventh floor. To get there I have to pass under a flickering light that's more off than on.

That's when I hear the noise. A kind of rustling, scuttling noise – but big, way bigger than a rat. I stand still, with my heart all **racy-fast**. The noise is near our car. I take a deep breath and tiptoe down the last five steps and out into the car park.

The fluorescent light **buzzes** and flickers off and I'm walking through the dark. There's that rustle again. I freeze. By now I'm nearer to the car than the steps. I make a **bolt** for it, pressing the unlock button so the car beeps and flashes just before I get to it. I haul open the back door, scramble over Baby's capsule and slam the door behind me.

I'm sitting on the baby wipes, listening to myself breathing. Whatever was out there knows I'm here.

A movement, a few cars away, catches my eye. A dark, shadowy, **dodging** movement. Like someone trying to hide. It reminds me of something. There it is again, ducking away behind another car. I realise what it reminds me of: myself, sneaking through the car park just now.

I watch. The flickering light comes on again and I see the person running. I grin. It's definitely a little kid, a kid darting away from me.

For some reason, that makes me want to give chase. I jump out of the car and the kid **bolts**. I run between the cars. There's the sound of a door closing and then nothing.

I look around. 'Hey! Where'd you go? Come out!' I call.

Nothing. **jeepers**, this kid must be scared.

'My name is Squishy Taylor,' I shout. 'I'm not going to hurt you.'

After another silence, a door I hadn't noticed creaks open and a voice says, 'What kind of a name is Squishy?'

It's a boy. I can see his sunburned face and dirty jumper.

'It's a good kind of name,' I say. 'It's like the gangster, only better.'

There was once a gangster called Squizzy Taylor, but that's not why I'm called Squishy. Mum and Dad gave me the nickname when I was little, because I used to squeeze between them when they were hugging. I'd wriggle in, yelling, 'Squish me! Squish me!' They got divorced ages ago, but they both still call me Squishy.

It could be an **embarrassing** name, so I'm lucky about the gangster.

The boy is in a cleaning storeroom, which I've never seen used before. As he steps out, I get a glimpse over his shoulder of a school backpack and a sleeping-bag laid out neatly on the floor. He pulls the door closed behind him.

'What are you doing here?' I ask.

'Nothing,' he says.

'That's not true,' I say.

'Well,' he shrugs, 'your real name's not Squishy.'

It's not. It's Sita, after my grandma, but Sita is only for the **serious-in-trouble** times. This boy doesn't need to know that.

We stare at each other.

'Have you got any food?' he asks.

'Well, dinner's nearly ready,' I say, but I know that's not what he means and he looks so sad that I feel sorry for him. 'You want me to sneak you some, later?' I ask.

He nods hard.

'How about we make a deal? I bring you food, and you tell me what you're doing.'

He looks torn, then says, 'Only if you promise not to tell **anyone**.'

I grin. 'Course!' I say. 'You're the best kind of secret there is.'

I remember something. I run to our car and grab the half-pack of rice-crackers (and the wipes) from the back seat.

I hand the food over. 'I'll have to wait until Dad and Alice and Baby are asleep before I sneak out, but these should keep you going.'

The boy grins. 'Thanks, Squishy Taylor,' he says.

'See you in the middle of the night!' I say, and run for the lift.

It's not till I'm at our apartment door that I realise I never asked his name.

Chapter Two

All through dinner, I'm burning with my secret.

Jessie and Vee aren't talking to me, but I don't care anymore. They sit down at the table in time, flicking their **twin ponytails** in time, scowling their **twin scowls**. Their mum Alice plonks spaghetti on the table while Dad gets everyone a glass of water.

Baby hits the table with his fat arms, drops broccoli on the floor and shouts.

This is what normal looks like now. I used to live with Mum, and Dad lived by himself. Then Dad moved in here, because of Alice having Baby. Then Mum got her job in Geneva and we decided I should stay here too. So now I've lived in Alice's apartment for seven and a half weeks and it's officially normal.

Dad told me that stepfamilies get a bad rap in fairy tales and maybe I should think of them as a bonus family instead. I don't think they're a bonus. They are about 95% annoying and 5% really, really annoying.

But tonight I don't care because I've got a secret.

I suck spaghetti strands and smile at my fork.

After dinner, I grab the iPad before Jessie can. She scowls but says nothing. The only time I don't have to fight for the iPad is when it's time to skype Mum. I lie on my tummy on the floor and push my curls out of my face.

'Hi, **Squishy-sweet**,' Mum says.

'Hi, Mum.'

'Let me just finish this sentence.' She starts typing. Mum's at work because it's daytime in Geneva. She finishes with a flamboyant full stop, then looks at me again. 'What'd you do today?' she asks.

'Um …' The first thing I think of is the boy downstairs, but if I told her about him she'd probably tell Dad.

'Um … I poured orange juice and flour in Vee's schoolbag this morning,' I say.

She groans. 'Oh great. Poor Alice.' But she has her sideways smile on. Mum was a rebel too, so she kind of likes that I am.

'You should have seen the **goop** it made,' I add, thinking gleefully of the dough all over her pencil case. 'It was all … **squishy!**'

She laughs. 'Probably not the best way to make friends with your stepsisters, hey?'

'I don't want to be *friends*! I've got friends at school. Did you know, Jessie spent an hour yesterday telling me how to do my homework –'

Just then, Jessie comes in. 'Hi, Devika,' she says to Mum, looking over my shoulder.

'Hi, Jessie,' Mum says.

'How's the UN?' Jessie asks, as if she's **100 years older** than me, rather than five and a half months.

'Oh,' Mum sighs. 'Bureaucratic. Huge. I don't know.'

Jessie waves at Mum and heads over to her telescope by the window.

'Well, how *are* your school friends?' Mum asks me. 'Bet they're all wishing you'd get on a plane to Geneva.'

I grin. My school friends are one of the main reasons I stayed. 'Nah. They're good.' But I don't really want to talk to her in front of Jessie. 'Love you,' I say.

'Love you too, Squish,' she says, and her picture slides away.

'Bedtime in seven and a half minutes!' Alice yells.

Vee does a **Kicking-Two-Jump-Scramble** up to the top bunk. She's such a show-off. Vee always invents new ways of getting up to the top bunk and then performs them like we should clap. When I try them, she does **bigger-kid-snob face** at me and pretends she's better. Which makes it way less fun.

Jessie takes the iPad off me without asking. She checks her telescope and makes notes in her astronomy app.

Then she folds her clothes into a neat square and slips into the bottom bunk.

'Goodnight, Vee,' Jessie says.

'Goodnight, Jessie,' Vee says.

They don't say anything to me. Which is kind of fair enough, since I made that **brilliant mess** in Vee's bag this morning. But that was fair enough, because Vee drew a moustache on my face with permanent marker while I was asleep last night. I got it off before school – but I had a red moustache until recess from the scrubbing.

Anyway. Whatever. I climb into the middle bunk between the twin-generated-silence and lie there. In the stupid **triple-bunk-bed** Alice built before I moved in.

I'm staying awake, thinking about my secret.

After ages, the line of light under our door goes out. I hear Dad and Alice's bedroom door close. Jessie and Vee are both doing sleep-breathing.

I slowly peel back the covers and tiptoe into the kitchen. It looks as though Dad or Alice discovered the secret stash of garlic bread and meatballs I hid under the table, but it's fine, they're just sitting in the top part of the bin. I grab an old take-away container and pile them in. Then I lift the key off the hook and ease open the front door.

When I get out into the corridor, I realise I don't just have to hide from Dad and Alice. I have to hide from every single adult in the building. Grown-ups take the responsibility of being grown-ups very seriously. Especially if they see kids in pyjamas out in the middle of the night.

Luckily, no-one spots me and I make it to the car park just fine. I tap gently on the boy's door. '**Room service**,' I say.

As he opens up, I hear the garage roller-door begin to beep and rise. Headlights shine down into the car park. He stumbles backwards and I follow him in, closing the door behind us.

'Thanks,' he says as I hand him the food. 'Hope they didn't notice the light.' He shoves a meatball into his mouth and we listen to the car pull up. We sit on his sleeping-bag with our backs to the wall.

'What's your name?' I ask.

'John,' he says, with his mouth full. 'John Smith.'

'Why are you here?' I ask.

'I'm hiding,' he says, taking a bite of garlic bread.

'No way!' I say sarcastically.

'From the police.'

I stop being sarcastic and do a **question-face** instead.

'I stole a tram,' he says. 'When the tram driver got out, I jumped in and drove it all the way to St Kilda. Now they want to put me in prison.'

'They don't put kids in prison,' I say.

I wish I'd stolen a tram.

I think for a little bit.

'Next time I'll do a secret knock, OK?' I say. 'Don't open to anyone except me.'

'OK,' he says. 'What will it sound like?'

I make up a really complicated knock that nobody else would *ever* do.

He shakes his head. 'I didn't get that. Do it again?' he asks.

But I can't remember it. I make up another one, but then I can't remember that either. It makes us both laugh. Finally we agree on a pretty quick and simple **tappety-tap-tap-tap**.

I stand up.

'Don't tell anyone I'm here,' he says.

'Course.'

'Will you bring food tomorrow night?' he asks. He suddenly sounds lonely.

'I'm going to bring you **so much food**,' I grin.

But when I open the door to leave, Vee is standing on the other side.

Chapter Three

'What are you *doing*?' Vee hisses.

John Smith is hiding behind me but he's pretty obvious. There's no point pretending.

'John Smith, this is my stepsister, Vee. Vee, this is John. He stole a tram and now he's on the run from the police.'

'You did not steal a tram,' Vee says,

but she sounds admiring. I can tell she wishes she stole a tram too.

John nods.

'I've been looking after him,' I declare, 'and I've promised to protect him with my life.'

I know that's not exactly what I promised, but John doesn't seem to mind and Vee looks a tiny bit impressed.

'I'll protect him too,' she says.

I want to say no and keep John Smith all to myself. I start to shake my head.

'With my life,' Vee adds, with her chin out.

I figure if she's not with me, she's against me. 'You can protect him,' I say slowly. 'But you're not allowed to tell Jessie. She'll tell the police for sure.'

John looks worried. 'Please don't tell,' he says.

Vee looks unsure, but I make her put one hand on her heart and the other hand on John's shoulder and look deep into his eyes and promise to protect him. I realise he really should have made me do this, so I do it too.

There's something very serious about it and I suddenly care even more that John doesn't get discovered.

Then we tell John we'll see him tomorrow and start for the lift.

'On **Pocket-Money Day**, let's buy him jelly snakes,' Vee says, as the lift starts climbing. Her voice sounds conspiring, like we're a team. It's kind of surprising and nice.

'Do you think we can sneak in before school?' I ask. 'The car park will be pretty busy.'

'One of us can be the decoy, while the other sneaks into his storeroom,' Vee says. 'What kind of decoy trick could we do?'

'Maybe we can set off the fire alarm,' I suggest.

Vee laughs. 'Maybe you can pretend to go crazy and sing opera and make everyone look at you.'

We make up lots of other stupid decoy tricks. Vee has never been this fun, ever. We are giggling so hard when we get to our floor that we totally forget to be quiet.

We would have remembered by the time we got to our door. But we have to go past Mr Hinkenbushel's first.

His door opens with a bang against the wall. 'What are you kids doing up at this time of night?' He's wearing old pyjamas and his face is red. 'You're keeping the whole building awake. What are your parents *thinking*?'

When he says 'parents', a bit of spit comes out of his mouth and flies across the hallway. I dodge it like a **ninja**, but that just makes him angrier.

'Where's your respect?' he shouts.

'Sorry, Mr Hinkenbushel, sorry,' Vee says and we duck away towards our place. He glares at us as I turn the key and then we're in. We close the door and lean against it, **whisper-giggling**. Vee's shoulder is warm, shaking against mine.

'How did you find me?' I ask.

'Not a problem,' Vee says. 'I was behind you from when you took the key.'

'You are so creepy!' I say and we burst into more giggles.

A door creaks open and Dad's sleepy voice bumbles in on our laughter. 'What are you doing?'

Chapter Four

While we make breakfast, Vee and I bump each other's shoulders and giggle. We're both trying to sneak food for John Smith, but there are too many people watching. Jessie is suspicious. She starts glancing sideways at me as she eats her cereal.

Alice is in the shower getting ready for work and Dad's trying to **bounce** Baby on his hip and make lunches at the same time. Baby is crying, squirming backwards and baffing Dad in the face with his fat little arm.

'Hey, Tom, how about I do that?' Vee says helpfully, taking the knife off Dad to spread mayo on the sandwiches.

Jessie stares at her like she's suddenly turned into a fake plastic fern. We never make our own lunches.

'Don't think you can wriggle out of your punishment for last night's **shenanigans**,' Dad says, but he sounds relieved and bounces Baby over to the other side of the room.

'Oh no, that's fine!' Vee says and I see she's **sneakily** making a fourth sandwich.

Last night, we managed to convince

Dad we only sneaked out as far as the kitchen for snacks. He was so happy I was getting along with Vee that he couldn't pretend to be angry for long. The lie should work as long as Mr Hinkenbushel doesn't tell. He probably won't. He doesn't like talking to grown-ups. He only likes shouting at kids.

I had the seriously **genius** idea for our punishment.

'We're looking forward to cleaning the car after school,' I say brightly. It's going to be hours where we can sneak in and out of John's storeroom, bring him food and ask him questions.

Jessie makes **snake-eyes** at me.

I realise I shouldn't look so happy. But it's too late.

'Maybe I can help you,' Jessie says sweetly.

Vee and I glance hopelessly at each other and then realise Jessie is watching us and we're giving ourselves away.

'That sounds great,' I say in a matching fake-nice voice.

Baby has started pulling Dad's hair with tiny, white-knuckled fists.

Dad and Baby walk us to the tram stop. There's a tall, scowly man in a neat blue coat standing there. He looks familiar but I can't tell why. I realise I'm staring and look away.

'Bye, Dad,' I say, as the tram pulls up.

'Bye, Tom,' say my stepsisters.

'Be good,' Dad says.

'And if you can't be good, be careful!' I call, from the tram step. It's something Mum used to say and it always makes me laugh.

'*What* is going *on*?' Jessie asks, as soon as the tram doors close.

'Nothing,' Vee and I chorus.

'**Don't lie**,' Jessie says.

'It's nothing,' Vee insists.

'We just got up together for leftovers last night,' I say, sounding innocent and nice, but really I'm rubbing it in. There's something fun about having Vee on my side for once.

'What, and now you're suddenly best

buddies and you want to clean the car together? You might as well pretend you got a job as an **astronaut**. I'm so onto you.' Jessie yanks her book out of her bag and sticks her nose in it.

I try to grin at Vee, but she looks worried. Jessie's lower lip is **trembling** and I don't think she's really reading.

She doesn't turn a page the whole way to school.

I'm in the year below, so I don't see my stepsisters all morning. At lunchtime, Vee pulls away from the older kids. She comes over to me and hisses, 'We just have to let Jessie help with the car.'

'Fine,' I snap, 'but you have to make sure your **spying** twin doesn't discover our secret.'

'Fine,' Vee says.

My friends look at me admiringly for talking so sharp. Until Dad and Alice got together, Jessie and Vee were just big kids at school who I never would have talked to. Now Vee and I are sharing a secret.

I'm halfway down the corridor with the vacuum cleaner when I remember we need the extension cord. Vee runs back to get it and then **Jessie-the-spy** says we should get a bucket and a cloth.

'Vee!' I yell. 'Get a bucket!'

Vee holds the door open with her foot and shouts back, 'Did you get a bin bag already?'

'No! Can you grab one?'

Next to us, the door opens. 'Will you kids shut the heck up?' Mr Hinkenbushel shouts.

He's so close it gives me a fright and I drop the vacuum cleaner. He stands and glares at us as I grab the handle and we drag our cleaning things to the lift. The extension cord gets caught in the door and I can't see properly because my curls are in my face. I look up and Mr Hinkenbushel smiles meanly.

The lift starts to go down and Jessie says, 'I hate him.'

I nod. 'Me too.'

We all stand there, **hating** Mr Hinkenbushel.

Once we start, cleaning the car is actually kind of fun and I forget Jessie is there to spy on us. Vee finds four dollars and promises to share. I find my old **ninja** sticker book from before Dad moved in with Alice. Jessie puts the little end on the vacuum cleaner and gets into all the corners. While she's got her head down, I do a quick run to the storeroom with the sandwich for John.

Tappety-tap-tap-tap.

As soon as he opens the door, I shove the sandwich into his hand. 'Can't stay,' I say. 'See you at midnight.'

Chapter Five

When the lift door opens at our floor, it's chaos. Mr Hinkenbushel is shouting at Alice and Alice is clutching Baby and shouting right back. Which is weird because Alice never shouts. Baby is screaming and Dad is trying to get everybody to calm down, hopping from one foot to the other like a **broken frog**.

'It's just plain rude!' Mr Hinkenbushel yells. 'What they need is boundaries, and you are clearly useless at providing –'

It turns out Mr Hinkenbushel likes yelling at everyone, including adults.

Alice is pale with **fury**. 'How dare you judge my family –'

'Now, Alice,' says Dad. 'Now, Mr Hinkenbushel ...' **(hop, hop, hop)**

They all stop like naughty children when they see us. Except Baby, who is still crying.

Alice coughs, trying not to look too crazy in front of us. Her voice turns cold and hard. 'Thank you for letting us know, Mr Hinkenbushel. Tom and I will have a *respectful* conversation with the children.' She turns on her heel and bounces Baby into the kitchen.

Vee leans into me as we drag the vacuum cleaner inside, whispering, 'But we were being *good*. We were cleaning the car.'

'That's it,' Alice announces, throwing herself down on the couch. 'I'm not cooking! If everyone thinks I'm a bad mum, I'll just be a bad mum!'

Dad gives her a shoulder squeeze and whispers something in her ear. She laughs, gets a big fat tear in each eye, and then gives her head a shake. 'Someone call the Curry Vault,' she says.

When it arrives, the roti is nothing like Mum's, but I don't complain. Dad winks at me over the dhal and I try to smile back. I even manage to shove some of the roti down my shirt for John Smith. Alice and Dad don't talk to us about Mr Hinkenbushel, but they're both very quiet. It's weird. Even Baby just sits there, smearing raita on a patch of table. Usually at dinner, someone is talking – even if the twins are both mad at me.

Vee does her homework without being asked, for the first time *ever*. I go and lean over her shoulder. 'I think only one of us should go down tonight. It'd suck to get caught.'

Vee bites her pen and nods.

I say, 'I'll go tonight because I found him. You can go tomorrow night.'

She turns around to argue with me, but I widen my eyes warningly. 'We can't argue now!' I whisper. I know I'm being

dramatic. But I'm kind of right, too. Alice and Dad are still all weird and tense and if we argue, they'll want to know why.

I grab the iPad before Jessie can, to skype Mum from bed.

Mum's working in her office and she looks busy, but she smiles at me anyway. 'Hi, Squishy.'

'Hi, Mum.'

'How was your dinner?'

'We had Curry Vault, with special **cardboard roti.**'

She laughs because 'cardboard roti' is her phrase.

'It was because Mr Hinkenbushel yelled at Alice,' I add.

Mum frowns. 'Your cranky next-door

neighbour? Well, I don't imagine Alice took that lying down.'

I grin. 'She didn't. She yelled right back.'

Mum does her funny sideways smile. 'Well, I'll say this for Tom, he's got good taste.' She's complimenting herself and Alice, more than Dad. Mum thinks Dad is pretty annoying, so annoying that she had to break up with him back when I was little. But she was happy when he found Alice, a girlfriend who was **smart** and **strong**. Mum likes Alice, especially now they're on opposite sides of the world.

Then I think about the tears in Alice's eyes tonight. I stop smiling.

'She said she was a bad mum,' I say.

'Well, that's a stupid thing to say.'

It's the same tone Mum uses when I tell her I can't do something. Half-irritated, half-supportive.

There's a pause.

I ask, 'If I wanted to, could I come to Geneva?'

Mum shifts her arms and leans in towards the screen. 'Sweetheart. Of course you can, if that's what you want ... But we did talk about it a lot.'

We did. I wanted to stay at my school. And Mum will be home in seven months and one week.

After goodnight kisses, I lie in my bunk in the dark, thinking about how

cranky Mr Hinkenbushel was and how horrible it is when he shouts.

'We should get him back,' I say. I don't need to tell Jessie and Vee who I'm talking about.

'I can't believe he shouted because we *washed the car*,' Vee says.

I know that's not really why he shouted. But anyway, it's not fair.

'Did you see Mum's face?' Jessie asks.

The bunk creaks and I can tell they are both rolling over, thinking about his **mean shouty voice** and her tears.

'We should do something to make him wish he didn't shout,' I say.

'Make him wish he'd never been born,' Vee agrees.

'Vengeance on our enemies,' Jessie says. She likes big words.

The Hinkenbushel Revenge Club,' I say.

Vee does a Rolling-Spin-Drop down to my bunk. 'Come on.' She drops again to Jessie. I follow down the ladder. I want to try Vee's bunk-bed move, but not in the dark when we're trying to be quiet.

We are all together on Jessie's bunk.

'Let's swear an oath,' Vee says. (I think she's inspired by swearing to protect John Smith.)

'Hands on,' Jessie says, and we knock shoulders and elbows as we shuffle our hands out onto the pillow.

'What should we swear?' I ask.

'To get back at Mr Hinkenbushel for

yelling at us and Mum, and to keep the club a secret forever and ever.'

'I swear,' I say.

'I swear,' says Vee.

'I swear,' says Jessie. Then she does a funny little hand wriggle. 'Boom! We are: the Hinkenbushel Revenge Club,' she says in a TV-announcer voice.

We all burst out laughing. It's funny how her announcer voice actually makes us feel like a team.

'Kids!' Alice calls from the lounge room. 'It's way past bedtime.'

We scramble to our own bunks and lie in bed, silent for a while. I'm thinking about how much fun Jessie has been tonight. Then I remember John Smith. I wonder if we told Jessie about him, it would be *more* of an adventure.

Jessie whispers, 'We could leave things on Mr Hinkenbushel's doorstep so he trips over them.'

'We could sneak up behind him and stick "kick me" notes on his back,' I suggest with a giggle in my throat.

'We could throw rotten fruit from our balcony to his balcony,' Vee says and we are all laughing again.

'Kids!' Alice shouts and we snort into our pillows.

I'm so happy, lying in the dark, laughing and trying to be quiet. For the first time ever, I think maybe my stepsisters *are* actually kind of a bonus.

I wait again until everyone is asleep and then tiptoe down to John Smith. As I press the lift button to get down to the basement, I start to wonder for the first time how John Smith got in there. The front door needs a swipe card and the garage roller-door needs a beeper.

The roti bread got a bit **smooshed** when I was lying on it, talking with Mum. But John looks pretty happy to eat something.

'How did you get in here?' I ask. 'Did you run in behind a car when the door went up?'

'Show you,' he grins.

He leads me down to the other end of the car park, where a little grate near the roof looks out at the footpath. He stands on the bonnet of the car in apartment 503's spot and reaches up to **jiggle** the grate. It pulls off in his hands. Then he hauls himself up through the hole. It looks a bit hard, but I think I can do it.

I **slither** up through the hole, out onto the street.

'This,' he gestures grandly, 'is my own personal bathroom.'

The old green public toilet is right opposite the grate.

'Aren't your parents worried about you?' I ask, suddenly worried about him myself. He can't hide in our basement forever.

'They don't care,' he mutters.

'They won't put you in jail,' I say. 'Not for borrowing a tram.'

'It'll be worse than jail,' John says.

I don't know how to answer that, so I just stand there for a bit.

'Vee and I are bringing you jelly snakes tomorrow,' I say. 'It's Saturday. **Pocket-Money Day.**'

I'm thinking hard. I bet his parents *are* worried. And I bet they don't want him to go to jail either. I need to find a way to talk it over with Vee.

Chapter Six

'Can I come to rock-climbing?' I ask, dipping **toast-fingers** into my egg.

Everyone stares at me. I never want to go rock-climbing because Saturday is Dad Day. But talking to Vee feels more important.

'Are you sure, sweetheart?' Dad asks.

I nod. It's perfect. Jessie will be at her violin lesson. I'm sure we can find a moment away from Alice.

Only problem is that the last time Alice suggested I come, Vee scowled. Later I found used teabags in my shoes. I swallow, waiting for her to say no.

'You'll need to tie back your hair,' Vee says.

I grin.

After breakfast Vee tries to help me pull the **masses of curls** up into a knotty ponytail. My hair springs around everywhere and we both start laughing. No-one knows how to deal with my hair except Mum.

I suddenly realise Jessie is doing **snake-eyes** at me again. I think she might hate it when I hang out with her twin. It gives me a mini sense of triumph.

We catch the tram together to Rockers, the rock-climbing centre, and Alice signs a piece of paper about me at the front desk.

'The **death form**,' Vee whispers in a **fake-scary** voice.

Vee helps me into the harness and then Alice checks it's all OK. The walls are really, really high, with little plastic knobbly bits in different colours going all the way to the top. There are heaps of other people along the wall at different heights, like flies.

I realise this was a fairly **drastic** plan for a way to talk to Vee.

Vee climbs first, and Alice shows me how to hold the rope to make sure she doesn't fall. She points out that Vee is using only one colour of knobbly bits. 'They're different levels of difficulty.'

I stare up at Vee. She's barely holding onto the wall with her fingertips! How can someone's fingers be so strong? She climbs higher and higher – almost to the roof.

By the time it's my turn I'm feeling **jittery**. What if I fall?

'I've got you,' Alice says, tugging the rope so it almost lifts me at the waist. I laugh, but it's a scared kind of laugh. I wonder if Vee can tell.

I start climbing. It's easy. My fingertips hold tight to the grips and I just clamber up, up, up. Looking for each new grip is fun and it's satisfying to feel my arms spread wide across the wall.

'I'm like a **ninja**!' I call, looking down.

Really bad move.

Alice and Vee are tiny. It's a long way to the floor.

What am I doing here? Why did I come? I don't even care about John or talking with Vee. I just care about not dying.

I'm frozen. My ears are buzzing. I realise that Vee and Alice are calling to me but I block them out. I just grip the wall and don't let go. My hands hurt. I need to wee.

The next thing I know, Vee is on the wall next to me. '**Freaking out?**' she grins.

And suddenly the world feels normal again. 'Not much,' I say.

'Let go of the wall,' she says. 'Mum can lower you down.'

Letting go feels like a really bad plan, but Alice gives me an encouraging tug on my harness. I **grit** my teeth and loosen my fingers. I swing into the air, but I don't fall – I stay right there. The harness feels a bit like a **hug**.

'If you hold this rope, you can lower yourself down,' Vee says. She shows me how to kick out from the wall and drift towards the ground. It's really fun. For some reason, having control feels safer than letting Alice do it.

'Can I have another go?' I ask as my feet hit the floor.

Alice laughs. 'Have a rest,' she says.

We watch Vee climb and then it's my turn.

This time climbing doesn't feel quite so easy, but I also don't freeze when I get to the top.

By the time it's over, my arms hurt and my fingers hurt, but I have a new favourite thing. I also realise that I've totally forgotten to talk with Vee about John.

Luckily, Alice makes it easy. She grins at us. 'How about this for a plan: you two catch your own tram home and I meet you there with lunch.'

'Really?' Vee asks.

'Give me a climb to myself and a cheeky hour in the office. You'll be fine. You catch the tram to school without me, don't you?'

This is true. But Jessie is usually with us and she's the responsible one.

I guess Alice thinks we're responsible enough without Jessie. And anyway, Jessie isn't *always* responsible. I think about her squeaky, **snorting** laugh into her pillow after we'd been told to be quiet.

Finally, the tram door closes and I've got Vee to myself.

'Do you reckon we should tell Jessie about John?' I ask.

Chapter Seven

I press B for 'basement' on the lift button, which means we aren't going to the park, and Jessie notices straight away.

'Where are we going?' she asks.

'We'll show you,' Vee grins. It's after lunch. We're taking Baby for his nap in the pram. He likes **walking-naps** and he's already asleep by the time we get to the lift, so this is going to be easy.

'What are we doing? Is it the HRC?' Jessie asks.

'What?' Vee doesn't get it.

'She means the **Hinkenbushel Revenge Club**,' I say to Vee. Then to Jessie, I add, 'No, it's not that. It's something just as important.'

We already checked with John on our way in and he said we could tell Jessie.

When we reach the car park, Vee is about to head straight for John's storeroom, but the scowly man from the tram stop is here. I grip Vee's arm. 'Hang on,' I say.

We watch as the man gets in the car from apartment 503 – the car under the secret exit. That would be why he looked familiar at the tram stop. I must have seen him in the lift. As he pulls out, I glimpse a dirty footprint on his bonnet. It makes me smile. The roller-door beeps down.

'All clear,' I say.

Vee pulls Jessie and I push Baby over to John Smith's storeroom door. I knock my special tappety-tap-tap-tap.

When John opens it, Jessie stares at him. He suddenly seems shorter when face to face with Jessie (which is weird because she's the same height as Vee). He looks a bit frightened.

'Who are you?' Jessie asks.

'His name's John Smith and he stole a tram and now he's in hiding from the police,' I say quickly.

'We're protecting him with our lives,' Vee explains.

The lift dings, announcing that someone else is arriving in the car park. We tumble into the storeroom before anyone sees us. Vee donks the pram on the doorframe, but Baby stays asleep.

'Your name's not John Smith,' Jessie pronounces.

The boy goes even whiter. 'How did you know?' he stutters.

'I know *now*,' Jessie says smugly.

We all stare at her. I realise she tricked him by **pretending** to know.

'Why did you choose John Smith anyway?' Jessie asks. 'It's the most obvious fake name in history.'

'Is it?' Not-John-Smith asks. 'I saw it on a TV show and I thought it was a good fake name.'

I'm a little bit angry. 'You lied! We brought you so much food and you lied to us.' I glare at him and Jessie. I'm annoyed that Jessie figured it out so quickly and I didn't.

'I bet you didn't even steal a tram either,' I say.

'Yeah!' Vee chimes in.

I'm just saying it because I want to make him feel bad, but his eyes go wide and I realise that was a lie too.

'You didn't steal a tram,' I say. 'You totally lied to us!'

He's biting his lip. 'I saw a story about it on the news. A boy did it and I wished it was me.'

I can tell Jessie feels sorry for him. 'It's part of the job of runaways to lie,'

Jessie says. 'They have to hide the real story to protect themselves. I bet the real story's even worse, isn't it?'

Not-John-Smith is looking teary and trying not to. Worse than stealing a tram and hiding from the police?

'What's your name then, Not-John?' I ask.

'If I tell you, you'll google me,' Not-John says.

Jessie grins and I realise she's probably going to google him anyway.

'Not-John is a good name,' I say.

Vee pulls the *jelly snakes* from on top of Baby. Baby makes his cutest noise and stays asleep.

'Why is there a baby?' Not-John asks.

'We stole him from a tram driver,'

Vee replies and we all giggle.

There's something about the sound of the jelly-snakes wrapper opening that makes me feel happy inside. We slide down to sitting on the floor, with the pram in between. Jessie passes the jelly snakes across the wheels to each of us.

'It's because of my dad,' Not-John says, biting the head off a **green** snake. 'We had a fight ...'

He looks angry and sad at the same time and his face nearly reminds me of something, but I'm not sure what.

'I want him to know I'm serious,' Not-John says. He looks serious.

'But you can't stay here forever,' Jessie says.

'Why not?' asks Not-John. 'I've got a bathroom.' He waves vaguely in the direction of the public toilet. 'Squishy Taylor feeds me. What's the problem?'

I imagine Not-John growing up, shaving in the green toilet and going to work every morning by climbing out the grate. I suddenly think of something.

'How did you even know to come here?' I ask. 'How did you know about the vent and the storeroom?'

Not-John looks down at his feet.

Jessie's mouth twitches. 'Did you run away from home to your own basement?' she asks.

Not-John doesn't say anything.

'**You totally did**!' Jessie says, sounding pleased with herself.

Baby rolls over and the pram squeaks.

I have a tingling feeling of dread and excitement. I bet I know who Not-John's dad is. I bet his dad is Mr Hinkenbushel.

Baby starts to cry.

'Your dad,' I start to say. 'Is he –'

Baby's wails get louder.

'Come on, Squishy,' Jessie says.

'But, Not-John's dad –'

'Squishy, we have to get out of here. The next person in the car park is going to hear screaming and wonder who's chained up in the storeroom.'

I stare at Jessie. She's right. And she's made me think of something.

'OK,' I say and let her pull us out.

Chapter Eight

'There's absolutely, one hundred per cent no way his dad is Mr Hinkenbushel,' Jessie says. 'That would mean there's been a kid living next door to us and we didn't notice. For years. No way.'

We are pushing Baby down to the playground because it's not time for his nap to finish yet. He likes the feel of his pram wheels rolling and he's already closed his eyes again.

'But what if,' I say excitedly, 'what if that's exactly why he ran away? What if Mr Hinkenbushel keeps him **chained up** in the cupboard?'

Vee looks nervous but Jessie snorts. 'He's got a schoolbag. And sunburn.'

'But Mr Hinkenbushel is so mean. That's exactly what he would do. It's probably why he's even meaner this week. Because his prisoner got away. And maybe it's not sunburn, it's a **skin disease.**'

Vee giggles and even I realise that's a bit silly.

'Well, whether he is or not, we still have to do revenge on him,' I say.

Jessie nods. 'He still hates us, and he shouted at Mum.'

At the playground, Vee and I shove the pram over to the monkey bars. Jessie sees another kid from school who's sitting in the corner-cubby with an iPad and joins her.

I show Vee my new monkey-bar moves. There's one really cool trick, where I swing **upside-down** from my knees and brush the pram with my hair. It's hard, because if you get it wrong, you either don't touch the pram or you bash your face on it.

Vee's impressed. 'You should do some bunk-bed tricks with me,' she says.

'OK,' I say, a bit surprised because of how much she hated me doing the same **bunk-bed acrobatics** before.

Baby wakes up screaming and we

have to run to get him home. Well, not run exactly, because we aren't allowed to run with Baby when we're next to the road. We just walk really, really fast. Kind of jog-walk.

As we get closer to home, we pass a massive dog out for a walk. I see the owner clutching a swinging plastic bag with a **squoogy-looking** weight in the bottom of it. And I have the best Hinkenbushel Revenge Club idea ever.

'Wait a sec,' I say to the others, as we pull up at our front door.

I trail the big dog and its owner until they reach the bin at the corner. As I suspected, the **squoogy** plastic bag is placed in the bin and the owner keeps walking.

I loiter beside the bin until the traffic lights change and the big dog crosses the road. Then I **snatch** the bag from the bin and run back to where Jessie and Vee are waiting for me. I wave the bag like a trophy. 'It's for the HRC!' I yell.

Vee and Jessie whoop and laugh.

When we get in the lift, the familiar scowly man is there too. Somehow, he's even more scowly than before. He looks at us and the pram, and the look in his eyes makes me wonder if he's not angry, he's sad. The others are glancing sideways at my bag and trying not to laugh, so they don't notice his face. He gets out on the fifth floor and as the doors close, the twins **collapse** with laughter.

Vee is clinging to the pram, flopping

over the side, and Baby grabs her hair so when she stands it makes him sit up. Then we laugh even harder and nearly forget to leave the lift.

But as soon as we do, I shush them. Mr Hinkenbushel's door is closed. Now's the time, before he comes home.

I crouch by Mr Hinkenbushel's doormat and tip the contents of the bag onto it.

'This is for you, Alice,' I whisper.

Wow. That was a **big** dog. Everything that dog did was big. I stare at the mound on Mr Hinkenbushel's doormat and then hurriedly stand up and back away. **Disgusting**. We pile into our place, giggling.

The HRC has made its first move.

Chapter Nine

I **roll** from the top bunk ...

Grab
the rail
with one
hand …
Swing and
kick my feet
out horizontal –

and then
land,
standing,
on the desk.

I have to steady myself against the wall, but Vee claps anyway from the top bunk. 'Awesome!' she says.

The whole bunk is still creaking and the telescope is rattling on its feet.

'Can you show me the next bit?' I ask, jumping down to the floor.

Vee follows me to the desk, but she doesn't stop there. She grabs the top of the wardrobe, **commando-rolls** across it only inches from the ceiling, and then kicks off the wall, returning to lying down flat on her bunk. The bed shakes wildly and I clap.

Jessie looks up from where she's reading the iPad on her bunk. 'There are no boys reported missing for this area in the last week,' she says. 'At least none who are Not-John's age.'

That stops Vee and I in our tracks.

'It must be Mr Hinkenbushel,' I say. 'He can't report it, because then they'll know he's been keeping prisoners.'

Jessie looks doubtful, but I'm starting to wonder if I might be right.

'I wonder if he's **trodden** in it yet,' Vee says and we all shriek with laughter. Vee does a **Quick-Drop** to the floor and then a **Kicking-Two-Jump-Scramble** back to her bunk. The wardrobe booms hard against the wall and a moment later, Alice appears in the doorway.

'Enough!' she says. 'I take you rock-climbing so I don't have to suffer this. Can't you do something very quiet for an hour? Like build a website? Sonja's boy builds websites and he doesn't make noises from one hour to the next.'

We spend the hours before dinner making an HRC website on the iPad. Jessie drives the iPad while Vee and I help by listing Mr Hinkenbushel's **crimes** and all the ways we're going to get him back.

While Jessie is doing the complicated bits, Vee and I take it in turns to look through the telescope at the boring people in the offices across the road. When the website is pretty much finished, we make a YouTube clip of us **'declaring vengeance'**, as Jessie puts it. It's awesome.

'Dinner!' Dad calls. We tumble into the kitchen. 'It's roll-your-own rice-paper rolls.'

The table is covered with lots of bowls of things cut up small. I pile my first roll with pork and satay. Yum. I add a little bit of carrot when Alice does an **eat-your-vegetables face** at me. There's too much pork and the whole thing falls apart, but I don't care.

I pick bits up with my fingers and smear them around the sauce on my plate. Alice seems to have got over being shouted at yesterday, and dinnertime is back to normal. Except that in the old normal,

Jessie and Vee weren't this nice to me.

'Is it Saturday-night movie night?' I ask.

Jessie is halfway through a neat roll. 'Can we download something new, pleeeease?' she asks.

'ßa-ba-ba,' says Baby, slamming a plate of cucumber sticks to the floor. We all laugh, including Baby, and I jump down to pick them up.

'Ten-second rule!' I shout as I gather the cucumber pieces together. It's not until I stand up again that I see there's something white sitting at the door. 'Hey, what's that?'

'What's what?' asks Dad.

'It's a piece of paper,' I say, going over to the door. 'That's weird.' We don't get paper under our door. Letters come to the letterbox downstairs in the foyer.

'Give it here,' Dad says, reaching for it, but not before I get a glimpse of the picture. It's Not-John, with 'MISSING' written in big letters across the top.

My heart slams into double-speed. I try to see over Dad's shoulder, but my eyes are jumping around, trying to read everything at once and not getting anything at all.

'There's a boy missing from the building,' Dad says.

Alice gasps and grabs her mouth. I don't think I've ever seen a grown-up look so scared.

'Apparently he left a note, and he's been

texting his dad pretending he's at his grandmother's.' Dad looks up at Alice. 'Sounds more like a runaway than a kidnapping.'

Alice's hand drops away from her mouth. She looks a bit relieved, but not much.

Dad keeps reading. Jessie and Vee and I can't help staring at each other.

'The note is from the boy's father, who only realised his son was missing when he talked to the grandmother ...' Dad checks the clock, '... an hour ago. But he's been gone for three days.'

'**Three days**.' Alice looks like she's going to cry. She grips Vee's hand, who's sitting next to her.

'He wants to know if anyone has seen his son.' Dad puts the note on the table.

None of us feel like eating.

'The poor man. He must be so terrified,' Alice says, pushing back her chair and taking the note. 'I'm going round to visit him right away.'

As soon as she opens the door, the whole apartment begins to smell of dog poo.

Chapter Ten

'We have to tell them,' Jessie hisses. We're stacking the dishwasher and putting uneaten food in the fridge. Dad is in the other room talking on the phone. Baby is sitting on the floor between us, **dribbling** chewed cucumber. The kitchen stinks and I'm seriously regretting our first HRC revenge attack.

'We can't keep Not-John a secret anymore,' Jessie whispers.

'But we promised!' I say. I remember staring into Not-John's eyes and swearing not to tell.

Vee looks torn. A promise is a promise. 'But if the dad is half as terrified as Alice –' she starts.

'But what if we're right? What if his dad *is* Mr Hinkenbushel? What if we need to protect him from his dad?' I say. I know I might be wrong. But I might also be right. 'We can't deliver him into the hands of his enemy.'

'Squishy, this is serious! Stop being stupid,' Jessie says in her most horrible grown-up tone.

I was serious. It just came out a bit

dramatic. I glare at her. 'I'm not being stupid! *You're* being a know-it-all goodie-goodie.'

Jessie comes over towards me but accidentally kicks Baby in the shoulder. Baby falls over onto one fat cheek and starts wailing.

'Look what you just did to my brother!' I say, and step forward to pick him up.

'*Your* brother? *Your* brother? He's *our* brother!' Vee says, teaming up with Jessie. Don't know why I'm surprised.

We all bend down, racing to pick him up first.

Bang! All three of our foreheads smash into each other. 'Ouch!' we all shout.

Jessie picks up Baby and stands shoulder to shoulder with Vee. They glare at me with **matching twin-glares**.

'Fine!' I yell. 'Have him! I don't even care. I don't even want him. Not if I have to live with stupid evil twinsies. And your stupid mum. I don't want any of you.'

My guts lurch, like something awful just happened. I wish I was in Geneva. I wish Mum never went to Geneva. I wish I could take back what I said and still be friends with Jessie and Vee. But I can't. I just said something really mean.

'What's going on, you lot?' Dad comes over, holding the phone away from his ear. 'Good grief, what's that smell?'

Vee is still clutching her forehead. 'It's **doggie-do**,' she says. 'Squishy left it on Mr Hinkenbushel's doormat and now it's everywhere.'

'You did *what?!*'

Baby struggles in Jessie's arms, crying. Dad is staring at me in horror. I am staring at Vee, feeling huge waves of **betrayal** roll over me. Also, my head is pounding where it got smashed.

'It was revenge!' I half-sob, half-shout. 'I did it because of how he yelled at your mum! You guys thought it was **funny**,' I plead, glancing at Jessie and Vee. Jessie still looks furious, but Vee is white. She looks like I feel.

'Dad …?' But I don't know what to say next. Which is weird.

Dad looks at me for a long moment. I think I see a kind of understanding in his eyes. There's a tinny voice coming out of his phone and finally he puts it to his ear. 'Sorry, mate, I'm going to have to call you back.'

'There's something else as well,' Jessie starts in her **know-it-all** voice. She's going to tell about Not-John.

'Not now, Jessie,' Dad says, taking Baby.

'But –' Jessie starts.

'Not –' Dad says.

'It's about –' Jessie tries again.

'Jessie, this is *not* the time.'

I've never heard Dad use that tone with anyone except me. It shocks me. It's like being in a parallel universe where I actually have a sister.

'Right now, I need to talk with Sita. Alone.' Dad only calls me Sita when things are really serious. He turns and walks into his and Alice's room.

I stare at Jessie, feeling sick. Vee told on me and I said something horrible. And now Jessie wants to tell on Not-John. I'm thinking of Not-John's white face. He said whatever was waiting for him was **worse than jail**. We can't break the promise we made him.

'Please, please don't tell yet,' I whisper. 'We promised.' I look at Vee, remembering the promise, and she looks undecided. But Jessie is stony. I try to bargain. 'Give me one hour. If it's not sorted out in an hour, I'll tell them myself.'

'Sita!' Dad calls in the kind of voice you can't ignore.

'Please …?' I beg.

Vee turns to Jessie. She's asking Jessie to wait too, with her eyes.

'Half an hour,' Jessie says grimly.

I spin and run in to Dad.

He says all the things. About how it was bad for Mr Hinkenbushel to shout at Alice, but that didn't mean it was OK to put dog poo on his doormat. About how he knows I must want to do funny things to make Jessie and Vee like me. About how he's glad I like Alice enough to want to protect her, but that she's quite capable of protecting herself.

'You know, Squisho, those two aren't just stepsisters.'

I can hear the 'bonus sisters' talk coming and I bite my lip and nod, thinking about how I just said Alice was stupid and that I didn't want Baby. I hate being told off when people are actually serious. Both Mum and Dad are a bit proud when I'm a rebel – I can hear the laugh of it in their voices. But Dad doesn't think anything is funny right now. And he won't stop talking. Every minute he keeps going is a minute less for me to get to Not-John and warn him to run away, or convince him to turn himself in.

'Are we clear?' Dad says finally.

I nod.

'Look at me, Sita,' he says. I look up into his eyes. 'I love you,' he says and pulls me into a hug.

'Dad?' I start, my mouth in his shoulder.

'Yeah, Squisho ...?'

'Can I run down and grab my silver jumper? I think I left it in the car.'

'Um. Sure.' He sounds a bit surprised, but lets me go.

I dash out into the kitchen. 'I'm going down to grab my silver jumper out of the car,' I say to Jessie and Vee, doing quote fingers, hoping they'll understand what I mean. I **bolt** out into the stinking corridor. The clock is ticking.

Chapter Eleven

I know it's probably faster to take the lift, but I can't bear to stand still. I pound down the stairs. The stairwell **stinks** for at least the first four floors. Has someone walked with dog poo on their shoe down every single corridor? Then I realise: of course someone did. Not-John's dad, with the 'missing' notice.

This is another piece of evidence that Mr Hinkenbushel is Not-John's dad.

What am I going to do if he is? I can't turn Not-John in to his dad if his dad is that horrible.

When I reach the bottom of the stairs, the car park is just as creepy as ever, but I can't care anymore. There's nobody else here. I **cannon** between the cars to Not-John's door and knock, forgetting any secret code.

He looks pleased to see me until he realises I didn't bring any food.

'Why did you run away?' I ask.

'Because I … my dad … he just … What's that **smell**?'

'Is your dad Mr Hinkenbushel and you ran away because he chained you in a cupboard your whole life?'

'Um … what are you talking about?'

Not-John is staring at me like I'm crazy.

'OK fine, I was wrong.' I'm almost disappointed, but then I realise it's a good thing Not-John's dad isn't that mean. 'So why did you say it will be worse than jail?'

'Because it's a **stepmum**!' he wails. 'My dad's got a new girlfriend and we're going to move in with her and my life is **OVER**.'

I just keep staring at him.

'What?' he asks. 'What's wrong?'

'You want me to protect you with my life against your **stepmum**?'

'Well, I didn't actually ask –'

'Have you met my stepfamily?' I interrupt.

'Well, yes … but that's different. You've

lived together forever, and you never fight,' Not-John says.

I laugh. 'Are you kidding?'

I think about the **horrible** thing I just said to my stepsisters and how Vee betrayed me. But I realise those things aren't even that important. 'You have to talk to your dad,' I say. 'He's talked to your grandma. The police are looking for you, and so is everyone in this building.'

Not-John goes pale and looks around the storeroom. 'I need to get out of here.'

'Maybe you should talk to your dad,' I say.

'He doesn't care.'

Not-John starts shoving things into his schoolbag. This is not going to plan. If he runs away, where we can't protect him, **anything** might happen. I think about his dad, who must be really worried. I remember how scared Alice looked when she heard a child was missing from the building. Not-John's father must be a **million** times more scared than that. I suddenly think how sad Mum was when I decided not to go to Geneva, and how much I love her. It gives me an idea.

'OK, OK,' I say. 'New plan. You pack your bag. Wait by the grate. I'll go outside and signal when it's safe to leave.' I pause, making things up. 'Um, there's three policemen out there, so you'll have to wait for me to distract them, and listen carefully for my signal.'

Not-John nods seriously.

I **bolt** to the lift.

'Dad, ring Alice,' I say, as I burst into the kitchen.

'What? Why?' Dad asks, turning towards me from where he is sitting with the twins. Jessie is sitting upright and Vee is sprawled back on her chair. They both look **sulky**, like Dad has been telling them off too.

'Quick,' I say. 'This is important.'

'But you said –'

'Dad! Call her!'

He starts rummaging for his phone.

I gesture at Jessie and Vee, pointing downwards and pulling a big anxious face, trying to make them understand how important this is.

Dad has found his phone, but he still isn't dialling. He's sitting there, looking at me. No wonder Mum broke up with him. **He's so hopeless.**

'Did Alice take her phone?' he asks.

The twins chorus, 'She always takes her phone!' and I can tell they are on my side, at least for now.

'What do I say?' he asks.

'Argh!' I snatch the phone and call her

myself. 'Alice, are you still with Not-Jo–the boy's dad? Yes? OK, meet us down the side of the building in seven minutes. Bring him. It's important.' Everyone is staring at me. 'Come on!' I say, as I push the phone back at Dad. 'There's no time!'

We all run out the door. Vee takes Baby from the rug and Jessie takes the key. Dad just flutters his arms around, saying, 'What? Who? Why?' and follows behind us.

Chapter Twelve

It's dark outside, which I had forgotten about, but luckily there's a streetlight just where I need it. I lead them to the bit of footpath near Not-John's secret grate. Then I stand right in front of it. I've got about five minutes before Alice turns up with Not-John's dad. Hopefully I can swing this before then.

'Um, while we wait, Jessie and Vee, I have to … um … apologise.'

I truly hope this works because it's **really, really embarrassing**.

'I'm sorry I said you were stupid and I didn't want any of you. Really sorry. It's not true.'

As I'm speaking, I realise I'm not just doing this to trick Not-John. I'm apologising because I've wanted to ever since the mean words burst out of me.

'I still wish you weren't such a **know-it-all** about everything,' I say to Jessie. But I say it in a light, teasy way.

'Can't help being smart,' she replies.

We look at each other and kind of smile.

I turn to Vee. 'And I'm still mad at you for laughing while I did the dog poo, and then telling on me like that.' Then I grin.

'But, turns out it was a **crappy** idea.'

Vee cracks a smile. 'Well, telling on people kind of **stinks**,' she says, and now we're all laughing except Dad, who's just standing there, holding Baby and looking a bit confused about why we're out on the street.

'And you know what?' I say to my stepsisters. 'You *are* a bonus. You're a **crazy-awesome bonus**.' I'm thinking about laughing in the lift and whispering late at night until we have to snort into our pillows. I'm thinking about Vee teaching me **bunk-bed tricks** and Jessie making us all do hands-on to join the HRC.

I take a deep breath. 'So I'm not going to call you stepsisters anymore.

From now on, you are my bonus sisters.'

It's just as cheesy as I thought, but no-one is looking at me like I'm an idiot. Jessie hugs me and Vee wraps her arms around from the other side and I'm squished in between them and it's perfect.

'What is going on?' Alice asks.

We pull apart. Alice walks up to us with the tall, scowly man in the neat blue coat. Except he's not wearing a coat today, he's wearing a brown knitted jumper.

I realise straight away why I always thought he looked familiar. He looks like Not-John. And he's got the same sad-angry face that Not-John has so much of the time. This guy is really not Mr Hinkenbushel. I feel desperately awful about keeping our secret from this poor man.

'Squishy?' Alice asks.

I look at Not-John's dad. 'It's about your kid,' I say. 'Um …' I cross my fingers, hoping this will work. 'How do you feel about him being gone?'

I step sideways so that when the man turns towards me, Not-John will be able to see his face from the grate.

Not-John's dad looks at me like I'm a crazy lady surrounded by a zoo. But he answers my question. 'I'm … I … he … I'm so afraid for him, I can't actually think.' His face is pale and serious with wide eyes. I was right. He looks more than just worried. He looks scared and alone.

There's a silence and I think maybe I've failed. I'm going to have to betray Not-John after all.

But then the grate behind me rattles and pushes out. There is Not-John's face at footpath level. He struggles onto his belly, then up and into his dad's arms.

I watch Not-John's feet kicking the air as his dad turns him slowly around on the spot, their faces hidden in each other's shoulders.

I feel a big, soft feeling of relief that they are together again.

We did it. Me and my **bonus sisters.**

We say goodbye to Not-John and his dad in the lift. Not-John tells us his real name but we don't care.

'You'll always be Not-John-Smith to us,' Vee says.

When the lift opens on our floor,

Mr Hinkenbushel is standing in the corridor looking furious.

He growls, 'What is this awful smell?

'I don't know,' says Jessie. 'It kinda smells **sweet** to me.'

Dad gives her a sideways look, but I can tell he's more laughing than angry.

When the door closes, I ask, 'Can we watch a movie now because it's Saturday night?'

'No,' Dad says.

'But you said –' Jessie starts.

'It's ten o'clock at night,' Dad says.

'But –' Vee says.

'Bed!' shouts Alice, and we scamper.

I do a quick **Running-Cross-Spin-Leap** into my bunk and nearly take out the telescope.

'You know,' I say, once the lights are off, 'I reckon Mr Hinkenbushel does keep prisoners **chained** in his cupboard. We just haven't discovered them yet.'

The End

For Lily Rose and Niamh – you've been
helping me think about stories since
you were tiny.

– Ailsa

For John. Thanks for trusting me.

– Ben

and a Question of Trust

Chapter One

I'm lying on my tummy with my eye **jammed** against the telescope so I can see into the building opposite. The office straight across from our bedroom belongs to Boring Lady. She's typing away as usual. Her face has no feelings on it.

But something is very wrong – she doesn't usually work in the middle of the night.

'What are you doing?' Vee grumbles in the bunk above me. It squeaks as she rolls over and my eye shifts against the telescope. We have a triple bunk-bed and I'm in the middle. It's awesome for **bunk-bed tricks** and the worst when you want to do night-time spying.

'Our bonus sister is being crazy as usual,' Jessie says from beneath me.

When I first moved in here, Dad said I should think of Jessie and Vee as a bonus. I thought he was just trying to make me feel better about moving in. But it turns out it's true: the twins mostly *are* a bonus. So we never say 'stepsister' anymore. Bonus sisters forever.

'I'm not being crazy,' I say. 'I'm watching Boring Lady.'

'But *Squishy*,' Jessie says. Everyone calls me Squishy, even my teachers. I'm Squishy Taylor – like the gangster Squizzy Taylor, only better. 'Squishy, it's the middle of the night. Boring Lady isn't working.'

'But that's the thing,' I say. 'She *is* working.'

'No way!'

Vee does her Rolling-Spin-Drop manoeuvre from the top bunk so she's lying beside me.

The telescope is ginormous and sits on a tripod. It's an old one from Alice, my bonus mum. Her university didn't want it anymore, so she gave it to Jessie. Jessie checks the stars and her astronomy app every night.

Vee has nudged me aside to look
through the telescope. 'No *way*!' she says
again, but this time she's not saying it
because she doesn't believe me.

'Guys!' Jessie says. 'Go back to sleep.
It's …' I can hear her rolling over to check.

'It's two fifty-seven in the morning.'

Vee doesn't move and her voice sounds kind of mushed from her cheek being pressed against the telescope. 'Boring Lady's just typing. Like she always is. Except it's two fifty-seven in the morning.'

'This is so weird,' I say. I love **weird stuff**. I wish there was more weird stuff in my life.

'This is so cool,' Vee says.

'Go back to bed,' Jessie says.

For twins, Jessie and Vee are pretty much opposites.

'I'll tell Mum,' Jessie threatens.

As if.

There's no way Jessie's going to wake up Alice. Not with Baby teething like he has been this week.

But Vee pushes away from the telescope. She drops down into Jessie's bed, gives her a growling tickly squeeze and then does the **Return-Leap-Roll**. It's a special jump we invented to get from the bottom bunk, up on the desk, across the top of the wardrobe and back onto the top bunk. It's pretty much a **ninja** move.

'Goodnight,' Vee says.

I push my curls out of the way to check the telescope again, but Boring Lady has finally packed up and left. Her office light is off.

I wonder if we should stop calling her Boring Lady now that she's done something kind of interesting.

I'm nearly asleep when I hear a

knocking, bumping kind of sound on the other side of the wall. **This is also weird**. Mr Hinkenbushel, who lives in the apartment next door, is supposed to be away for work for the next month.

Chapter Two

In the morning, I wake up to the smell of smoke and the sound of screams. I do a **Drop-to-Running** descent (always the quickest way out of my bunk) and am in the kitchen pretty much before I'm awake.

The **smoke** is from Dad burning crepes and the **screams** are from Baby, who is unusually angry this morning.

'Here,' Dad says and thrusts the flipper

towards me. Then he picks up Baby from his rug. Baby stops crying.

I loosen the edge of the crepe and then flip it. I'm an **expert crepe-flipper**.

'Thanks, Squish,' Dad says.

It's not until later, when we're sitting around the table having breakfast, that I remember the noises next door. I get the yucky feeling in my chest that I always get when I think about Mr Hinkenbushel.

'Mr Hinkenbushel came home early!' I announce.

'Oh no,' Vee says.

Mr Hinkenbushel hates us and we kind of hate him right back. One rainy day when we were riding our scooters down the corridor, he called us '**idiot kids**' and his face went all red and he spat by accident from the yelling. Another time he even shouted at Alice. We were so mad at him – that's when we declared **vengeance** on him.

'How do you know he's back?' Jessie asks.

Vee looks up from tipping about a litre of maple syrup on her crepe.

I tell everyone about the noises in the night, but I can tell they don't really believe me.

'He said he wouldn't be back until next month,' Alice says. As though that settles it.

'We'll have to re-start the HRC,' I whisper to Vee, but Dad hears me and glares. '**JOKES!**' I say, throwing my hands in the air.

HRC stands for **Hinkenbushel Revenge Club**. The club was my idea. It was the first really fun thing I did with Vee and Jessie after I moved in (apart from harbouring a runaway in our basement, which kind of happened at the same time). Jessie built the HRC website. We even made a revenge declaration video, which got twenty-five hits on YouTube. We started the club when Mr Hinkenbushel shouted at Alice, so she should have been grateful. But she wasn't. Our first revenge act massively **backfired** and Alice and Dad were both pretty mad about it.

It's probably lucky they never found out about the website.

And now Mr Hinkenbushel is back,

which sucks. It's so boring to have to be quiet every time you leave the house.

'All right, you lot,' Dad says. 'This is your half-hour call.'

It's Saturday. That means Alice is taking me and Vee to rock-climbing while Jessie does violin, and Dad and Baby clean the house.

Rock-climbing is my new favourite thing. Mum sent me climbing clothes from Geneva after I told her I was doing it: three-quarter-length galaxy-print leggings and a silver sports top. I like the top because it has a cross-back that makes my shoulders look strong.

I scramble my curls into a fat, high ponytail to keep them out of my eyes. When I'm done, I lean against the window, looking out at Boring Lady's desk. I can tell there's no-one there, even without the telescope. I wonder what she was doing last night. Maybe it wasn't so strange after all. Maybe Boring Lady always types at 2.57 in the morning – it's just that I'm not normally looking?

Jessie is lying on her bunk with the iPad, reading the news. That's one of the weirdly grown-up things Jessie does.

'Pyjamas,' she says, as I'm about to leave them in a pu**ddle** on the floor. For ten years, I had my own bedroom when I lived with my mum. I used to leave my pyjamas wherever I wanted and Mum would just laugh at me. I could have moved to Geneva when Mum got her job there with the UN. Instead I moved in with Dad and Baby and our bonus family. Mostly a good choice – until Jessie starts telling me what to do.

I lean over Jessie to shove my pyjamas under my doona. She taps the iPad and a lazy, posh, English-sounding man says, *'It's absurd to suggest these diamond smugglers are operating in Melbourne. All one has to do is look at a map!'*

Diamond smugglers? Cool. I'm almost tempted to look at whatever Jessie is listening to.

But then Alice yells from the kitchen, 'Climbers! Time to leave!'

I follow her and Vee out into the corridor. They're both wearing cross-back tops too. Alice's is grey and Vee's is hot pink. Their shiny black ponytails swing in time as they walk.

On the way past I see that Mr Hinkenbushel's door is slightly open. This is a bit weird – his door is usually

double-locked – so I can't help glancing in. It's really messy inside. I wonder if he got home and just tipped his suitcase all over the floor.

I stand still for a moment. **Unless he's been burgled?** There's a bright page from a magazine lying half out the door. It doesn't look like the kind of thing Mr Hinkenbushel would have, so I lean down to pick it up.

'Alice …?' I call, wanting to tell her about the mess. But they're straining to hold the lift open with their hands, because the 'stay open' button is broken.

I laugh and **bolt** for the lift.

Chapter Three

'Bet I can climb the Gargoyle's Escape,'
Vee says as we push through the big glass
doors into Rockers, the rock-climbing
gym. Vee always says that, but she still
can't do it.

'Bet you can't,' I say.

'Bet *you* can't,' Vee says back.

Alice is the only one of us who's ever
climbed the Gargoyle's Escape. It's the
hardest section of the wall.

Rockers has a huge glass wall, so you can look out at the city if your fingers are **gripping** tight enough. I've only been climbing for a couple of weeks, but I'm almost as good as Vee already. When it's my turn, I climb fast. Sometimes when I'm climbing, I have to be really strategic, and plan where to go next. But sometimes, like today, the holds seem to just appear without me thinking about it. It's like my fingers and arms are working without my brain noticing. The other cool thing about rock-climbing is it makes you better at **monkey bars** and **bunk-bed acrobatics**.

We take it in turns to climb or belay (holding the safety rope for the other person) till our arm muscles ache.

Alice gives us smoothie money and sends us to catch the tram home alone while she goes on to work.

We always race for the shower, so when we get back Vee shoves past me into the kitchen, trying to beat me there. But there's a policeman sitting at the table. Vee stops and I bump into her back. Dad is frowning at the policeman.

'Whoa there, little ladies!' says the policeman, like he's talking to some kind of pony. He chuckles as though we are adorable and stupid.

I stare at him.

'Veronica, Sita,' Dad says, 'this is Constable Graham.' Dad only calls me Sita when something is important. It makes me a bit scared.

'What's going on?' I ask.

'Nothing, nothing,' Constable Graham says, resting his hands comfortably on his stomach. 'There's some kind of problem next door, so I'm talking to all the neighbours.'

I think of the noises in Mr Hinkenbushel's apartment last night, and remember the mess I saw this morning.

'Did Mr Hinkenbushel get burgled?' I ask. I nearly add, 'Serves him right,' and I think Dad hears my thoughts. He glares at me.

'*We*-ell,' the policeman says. 'I wouldn't say burgled, exactly. Not exactly. Ms Kuot across the corridor called us because she saw the mess. We tracked down Mr Hinkenbushel on the phone this morning. He's still away and we located his list of valuables. None of them are missing. So it's looking like a break-and-enter. Vandalism.'

Vee and I stare at each other. A crime on our very own floor. This is cooler than a lady typing at night.

'You two **princesses** haven't seen anything suspicious, have you?' the policeman asks. 'Anyone hanging around here who might have done it? Some **bigger boys** maybe?'

Princesses! Bigger boys! I want to **choke**.

'Squishy – I mean, Sita – heard a noise last night,' Vee says.

So I tell him about the noise and how I know it was after 2.57 because of

Jessie checking the time. He nods and notes it on his iPad. Jessie arrives in the middle of it, with her violin slung over her shoulder. She agrees about when she checked the time.

'Good. Good to know.' The policeman stands up and smiles at me like my prep teacher used to. 'You've been very helpful, Sita.' Then he chuckles. 'Or should I say, Squishy?'

He's laughing at me. It doesn't feel very nice.

He shakes Dad's hand and then does a **stupid little wave** at us kids, like we're two-year-olds.

Dad closes the door with a solid click and turns back. His face is very, very serious. 'OK, you lot. If this has anything to do with that ridiculous club of yours, tell me now.'

The Hinkenbushel Revenge Club. We **wish** we broke into his apartment!

'Of course not,' Jessie says. 'That was only a game.'

'We quit exactly when you told us to,' Vee adds.

'It *really* wasn't us, Dad,' I say.

He looks us in the eyes, one by one. 'If you own up now, it's much better than being caught later.'

We all look right back at him. He seems satisfied.

Then Baby wakes up and starts crying and Jessie goes to put her violin away. Vee beats me to the shower. I stand in the kitchen, thinking.

I remember the piece of paper I picked up from Mr Hinkenbushel's doorway and dig around in my bag to pull it out. I unfold it and spread it on the table.

It's a catalogue for very **expensive** diamond rings.

Chapter Four

It's pizza for dinner so we are all helping. Vee is smearing tomato sauce over the bases, Jessie is neatly laying out mushrooms, salami and olives, and I'm grating cheese for the top (and eating **pinches** of it as I go). Alice is in charge of the oven and Dad is in charge of Baby.

The news is on. *'Police are closing in on a diamond-smuggling operation, which*

sources say is operating somewhere in central Melbourne. Lord Smiggenbotham-Chancery has been helping with the investigation.'

Then a familiar lazy posh voice comes on. *'These criminals will stop at nothing. The Australian Police should be very afraid.'*

I think about our policeman and grin.

'Do you think Constable Graham is "very afraid"?' I ask, helping myself to more cheese. Vee slaps my hand with the sauce spoon and tomato splatters everywhere. We try not to giggle. Vee makes a tiny gesture, pointing to a spray of sauce on Alice's shirt, and we both try even harder not to giggle.

The reporter's voice comes back on.

'*Police are seeking forged documents that declare the diamonds to be legal.*'

'What makes diamonds legal or illegal?' I ask.

'Well, that's a good question for your mother,' Dad says. 'Ask her next time you skype.'

'OK.' Mum is better at answering questions anyway.

'Oh, damn!' Alice says, and I think she's found the splatter on her shirt. But it's not that. 'I forgot the mangos,' Alice says.

Vee and I groan **dramatically**. We only get dessert on Saturday nights. It's one of the **dumb** rules my bonus family brought in.

'Maybe we could go down to the

corner and get a tub of ice-cream?' Jessie asks. That's the thing about Jessie. She knows when to ask for things.

Alice hesitates and then sees all the pizzas, neatly lined up and ready to go into the oven. 'All right,' she says, and reaches for her wallet.

The three of us race out the door and head towards the lift. We bang straight into Mr Hinkenbushel.

'Oi! Watch where you're going, can't you? Lousy kids.' Mr Hinkenbushel has messy hair and his jacket is all crumpled. He's scowling at us.

'Sorry,' we chorus and then run for the lift. As the lift door closes, I see Mr Hinkenbushel put his key into the lock and open his apartment door.

We stare at each other. He really is back!

We fight over whether to get chocolate or salted caramel, and Jessie wins because she's carrying the money. When we get home, we **tiptoe** past Mr Hinkenbushel's door, but we may as well not have bothered because he's standing in the kitchen with Alice.

'Yes, my plane arrived this afternoon,' Mr Hinkenbushel is saying. 'I thought I'd better come home and get the place sorted out.'

Alice and Dad are nodding with **sympathetic faces**.

I push his diamond catalogue deeper into my pocket as Jessie edges past with the ice-cream to get it to the freezer.

The room smells like hot melted cheese and I remember how hungry I am.

When Mr Hinkenbushel leaves, **scowling**, Vee sticks out her tongue at his back. Dad gives her a warning look. I pull pieces of salami off my pizza and eat them thoughtfully.

'Did Mr Hinkenbushel say he just got back?' I ask.

Dad nods.

'Like, just this second, on the plane?' I need to get this right.

Dad nods again.

I see the image of Mr Hinkenbushel unlocking his apartment as we got into the lift. 'But he didn't have any luggage!' I cry.

Dad and Alice don't seem to care.

But I know what my mum looks like when she gets off a plane. She always has at least two bags, one of them a big suitcase on wheels. Mr Hinkenbushel was carrying *nothing*.

After dinner, I skype Mum on my bed.

'Hi, my **Squishy-sweet**,' she says. She's in her office because it's daytime in Geneva. She tries not to be busy at my bedtime. 'What's happening?'

'The news says there are illegal diamonds in Melbourne. Why would they be illegal?' I ask.

'Well ...' she starts. One thing I love about my mum is that she takes my questions seriously. 'There are two reasons. Firstly, because in some countries, diamond miners are paid very badly and work in terrible conditions. So other countries try to help the miners by making it illegal to buy those diamonds.'

I understand why Dad said to ask Mum. Her work is all about countries working together to make everybody's lives better. That's what she's trying to do at the UN.

'And secondly, because when you bring diamonds into Australia, you have to pay tax. So some people smuggle them in, to hide from the tax office. Which means they make more money. It's greedy.'

I nod. It makes me think of the shiny diamond catalogue in my pocket. The one

I found on Mr Hinkenbushel's doorstep. Why would Mr Hinkenbushel even have a diamond catalogue? Unless ...

I hold the excitement in my chest while I say goodbye to Mum and while Jessie and Vee come to bed. Dad and Alice kiss us, and close our door. Then I make Jessie and Vee come sit on my bunk and whisper.

'It's Mr Hinkenbushel. He's the **diamond smuggler**.'

They both laugh at me but I poke them. 'No, listen,' I say. 'He had no luggage just now. Why would he have no luggage? Because he was already back!'

'What?' Jessie scoffs. 'He was just hanging out with the burglars?' Then she pauses thoughtfully.

I nod, even though they can't see me in the dark. 'He broke into his own apartment to make it look like he wasn't there. That's why nothing was stolen!' I can feel my voice getting louder and I have to make myself calm down so Dad and Alice don't hear us. 'Plus, I found this.' I hold up the diamond catalogue and shine the iPad light on it. 'It was in his doorway. Why would he have this?'

Jessie takes the catalogue off me and turns it over. It sparkles under the light. She seems interested, but not convinced.

'Anyway,' I say, 'do you know what his job is?'

Both of them shake their heads. I don't know either. We stare at each other across the iPad light. Why would Mr Hinkenbushel keep his job a secret? That's pretty suspicious.

Vee starts to get excited. 'A real-life **diamond smuggler**!' she says. 'Cool.'

'You'll have to be able to prove it, though,' Jessie says.

'We have to tell the police,' I say.

Chapter Five

The next morning, I announce to Dad that we need to go to the police. Baby is screaming on the change table in the bathroom, and Vee and Alice are in the kitchen **fighting** about homework. Vee and Alice are the only ones who ever fight about homework. Jessie does hers because she *likes* it and Dad just forgets about mine. Alice says she'll cook for me and wash my clothes, but she won't make me do my homework. This is **fine** with me.

'Mr Hinkenbushel is the diamond smuggler, Dad,' I say, over the noise of Baby crying.

Dad wipes poo off Baby's kicking legs. 'What diamond smuggler?' he asks.

'The one on the news! Haven't you been listening? There's a Lord from England trying to find him and he's in Melbourne and we know it's Mr Hinkenbushel. We have to tell the police.'

Alice's voice gets louder in the other room. 'Just **focus**, Veronica. You could finish this in half an hour if you tried. You're not **trying**.'

Dad smears some cream onto Baby's bottom, which makes him scream even louder.

'So, can we go to the police?' I ask.

'No,' Dad says. Just like that. I don't think he even heard me properly.

'But Dad –'

'No, Sita.'

'But you didn't even –'

In the other room, Vee yells, 'MUM! I'M TRYING TO TELL YOU! SHE NEVER EXPLAINED IT TO ME.'

'Do something useful and play with your brother,' Dad says and puts Baby into my arms. Baby stops crying and reaches around my neck.

Dad takes my shoulders and turns me towards my bedroom. I hear him talking as he steps into the kitchen. 'Cup of tea, Alice?'

Jessie is in our room on the bottom bunk. She's lying on her tummy, looking at the iPad. I plop Baby on his back next to her and he starts pulling her hair and giggling.

'No-one will believe you,' she says. 'You don't have any evidence.'

She nudges her nose up to Baby's and nuzzles it from side to side. He gurgles and his smile gets even bigger. He's pretty cute.

'But the police station's only round the corner,' Jessie says. 'We could just go.'

She shows me the map. She's already done a search and we don't even need to cross a road to get there.

Alice says we can take Baby for his nap (he always goes walking for his nap) but she makes us tell her the three rules:

1. **Be quiet in the corridor.**
2. **Don't cross any roads.**
3. **Never let go of the pram.**

We know them off by heart.

Vee **glares** at us and we grin back. She knows we're up to something fun but she can't come with us. She has to finish her project.

Baby is asleep before we get to the lift. The police station is four doors down from the ice-cream shop. I do **One-Foot-Slide-Scoots** with the pram

down the hill and
Jessie tries to
stop me.

I figure
it's not dangerous,
though, because I obey rule number
three: I never let go of the pram.

As we get close to the police station door, I start to feel nervous.

Inside there's a big glass window with a little hole in it. I almost wish we didn't come. A policeman steps up behind the counter. He is younger than Constable Graham and has a big smile.

'What's going on, guys?' he asks, **grinning**. 'D'you find a baby?'

'No, he's ours,' I say.

'Let me guess ... you're the father?' He points at me and we all laugh.

When we stop laughing, Jessie speaks. 'We're here about the diamond smuggler.'

'Oh-kaaaay,' the policeman says. 'Hang on a minute.' He types something into his computer.

'So, talk to me,' he says.

Jessie nudges me. So I tell him about Mr Hinkenbushel having no luggage and how he wasn't away at all, so he must have faked the burglary himself. I show the policeman the diamond catalogue I found. His lips are pinched together, like he's trying not to laugh, but he types it all down.

'Is that everything?' he asks.

I think about what the news said – the police are looking for forged documents that declare the diamonds to be legal.

'Well, Mr Hinkenbushel probably has the forged documents. They'd be in his apartment. Or a secure bank safe,' I say. 'Or maybe buried somewhere.'

His face cracks into a huge smile, like I'm the funniest thing he's ever seen, but he's nice anyway. 'OK. Well listen, thanks for coming in.' His face goes serious. 'It's really important to report **suspicious** things. Even if they feel a bit … silly.'

He doesn't believe us.

Out on the street, Jessie pushes Baby and I climb up and walk the fence rail by the church. I can usually take seven steps before I have to jump down, but this time I only get to three. I hate that the policeman doesn't trust us.

Chapter Six

After school on Monday, we all catch the tram home. Before I had a bonus family, Mum or Dad picked me up. Now that there's three of us, we catch the tram. Alice says we can look after each other.

The tram is empty enough to do **Upside-Down-Crazy-Legs** from the handholds, but Vee won't join me. She's mad at us for going to the police station without her.

I do twenty-five scissor kicks and don't even let go when the tram stops. 'Bet you can't do that,' I say to Vee, stumbling down to my feet and nearly falling on her.

She does thirty-two and then sits with her back to me.

Jessie rolls her eyes at me and whispers, 'She's been like this all day.'

Jessie reminds us in the lift to be quiet going past Mr Hinkenbushel's door. Not that we were making any noise anyway. I slow down as we pass, but Mr Hinkenbushel's door is closed and I feel a bit disappointed. Maybe nothing has happened.

I'm ready for snacks and a massive glass of milk, so I open our door with my key and **barge** into the kitchen first.

Then: 'Whoa there!' says a familiar voice.

Constable Graham is sitting at the table with Dad and Alice. None of them look very happy. They've got the iPad in front of them and when I see what they're looking at, I feel sick.

It's the HRC website with our old **revenge** video.

They've paused the video halfway through. My face is close to the camera. My nose is wrinkled and my eyes are squinty.

'Sita,' Dad says. 'What were you *thinking*?' He sounds angry and disappointed and I stare down at the iPad screen.

Constable Graham taps a stumpy finger on the iPad and the video starts playing again. It's me, talking (but Jessie helped make up the words): *'So, in conclusion, we swear dire vengeance on Mr Hinkenbushel. Anything we can do to make his life worse, we will. We will strike him down, mess him up and turn his world inside out.'*

Then Vee and Jessie squash their faces next to mine.

'We swear,' they both say, pulling snake-eyes at the camera.

'We're gonna get you, Mr Hinkenbushel!' I promise.

Then Jessie reaches forward to stop

recording. As she does, you can hear us all start to laugh.

There is silence in the kitchen.

Constable Graham says, 'It was you three who broke into Mr Hinkenbushel's apartment the other night, wasn't it?'

Jessie has gone white and is shaking her head.

'No!' I say. 'We would never!'

'Well, *I* didn't,' Vee says, and you can already tell she's going to say something mean. 'But I don't know what Jessie and Squish have been doing …'

As if we could have broken into Mr Hinkenbushel's without her knowing.

'It really, *really* wasn't us, Dad,' I say.

Dad shakes his head and gestures towards the iPad. 'This video is plenty to get you into trouble, Sita. **It's a question of trust**. You went and put this online after you *promised* you'd give up that club.'

'But we did give up the club. This is from before. We haven't looked at it for *months*. We'd pretty much *forgotten* about it. *Really*, Dad.'

'It's true,' Jessie chips in. 'It says it on the YouTube page.'

Dad holds up his hand. '*Enough*, Jessie. Constable Graham wants to speak with each of you, one at a time. Jessie first. Vee, go sit in your room. Squishy, our room.'

They're separating us because they don't **trust** us. They think if we're together, we'll make up lies. For some reason that makes me feel worse than anything that's happened so far. I feel the tears choking in the back of my throat and run before everyone sees.

I lie on Alice and Dad's bed, crying into my hands. I wonder what the policeman is going to say to me. I hate that Dad thinks we'd lie to him about something this big. I wish Vee wasn't so mad at us. I wish my mum was here. I look around for the iPad, thinking about skyping her, but it's busy being evidence in the kitchen.

I roll over and look over Dad and Alice's balcony to the building opposite.

Boring Lady is in her office. Typing as usual.

I get up and go out onto the balcony. I look along our outside wall. If I lean out far enough, I can almost see into our bedroom. I wish I could talk to Vee, make her understand that we didn't want to leave her out when we went to the police. Make sure she doesn't say some dumb lie and get us all in trouble. If I was really desperate, I think, I could swing myself across to our window. I measure the handholds with my eyes as if I was at the rock-climbing gym.

Then Dad calls from the kitchen and I realise I've accidentally locked the balcony door behind me. It doesn't matter, because I can do the **bobby-pin trick**. The locks on these balcony doors are pretty simple because being eleven storeys up is its own security.

I pull a pin out of my hair and click it

easily in the lock. But the bobby-pin trick isn't as fun and satisfying as it usually is. My stomach has dropped down so far it's pretty much on the floor. I don't want to talk to the police.

Chapter Seven

By the time Constable Graham finally leaves, Dad believes that we didn't break into Mr Hinkenbushel's apartment. So does Alice. Vee obviously didn't make up any lies about us, but she's just as obviously still mad. And Dad and Alice are **really mad** about the website and the video. They talk seriously about online bullying and community spirit.

They should talk to Mr Hinkenbushel about community spirit. He's the one who shouts and won't let us play in the corridor. And probably **smuggles illegal diamonds**.

Dad skypes Mum and they talk for ages. Then Mum doesn't have time to talk to me before she has to race off to her next meeting. That doesn't feel fair. The one time I really need to talk to her, and Dad gets all the time she has.

I lie in bed in the dark, thinking about Mr Hinkenbushel. I wonder if the police are any closer to figuring out that he's their man. Probably not. They're too worried about me and my bonus sisters being criminals. Still.

'How are we going to catch Mr Hinkenbushel?' I whisper.

'Go to sleep,' says Jessie, in the bunk underneath me.

'No-one's going to believe us now,' I whisper.

'That's because you don't have any evidence,' Jessie says.

'Serves you right for not taking me to the police station,' Vee says, rolling over sulkily, making the whole bunk shake.

'That's got nothing to do with it,' says Jessie.

There is a pause.

'It was still mean, though.'

'Well, if you'd done your homework when you were supposed to –'

'Shut UP, Jessie. We can't all be boring losers,' Vee half-shouts. I can tell she's sitting up.

Dad's voice growls warningly from outside, 'I can hear you, kids.'

The room echoes with offended silence.

'We just have to find the evidence,' I say.

But no-one answers.

In the morning, Vee isn't talking to any of us. Jessie turns on the radio news while we all eat cereal. It's boring. I try to hold

Baby on my lap and eat at the same time, but I **drop yoghurt** on his head and Alice takes him off me.

Then it's the story we've been waiting for.

'*Sources say police are still seeking forged documents that they hope will lead them to the diamond smugglers. Lord Smiggenbotham-Chancery suggests Melbourne Police might not be up to scratch.*'

The familiar, lazy voice comes on. He sounds half-amused. '*The police department is the most bumbling, absurd, inefficient force I've ever had the displeasure of working with.*'

Then the reporter comes back on. '*The government says it is not considering an inquiry into police productivity at this stage.'*

Jessie meets my eye over her breakfast spoon. She's thinking what I'm thinking. Those forged documents might be just the **evidence** we need against Mr Hinkenbushel. She's smart enough not to say anything in front of Dad and Alice. Also, there's the problem of Vee.

Vee gets on the tram at the opposite end to us. She sits there with her earphones in and her ponytail swinging. Jessie rolls her eyes.

I lean in to Jessie and whisper, 'If Mr

Hinkenbushel has the forged documents, where do you think he's keeping them?'

Jessie shrugs, her eyes on Vee's ponytail. Finally she says, 'We need to know what he does, where he goes, understand his movements. But ...'

I know what she's thinking. If we get any further into this adventure without Vee, she's going to be so mad she might **blow up our apartment** – or the whole of Melbourne.

'There's only one thing for it,' I say finally. 'A crazy bonus-sister apology.'

I stand up on the crowded tram and shout out, 'I'm **SOOO** sorry, Vee!'

She looks around. First success. I was louder than the music in her earphones. She **scowls** and shrinks down in her seat. I push down the aisle towards her, **donking** people with my schoolbag on the way through. Jessie follows, giggling and trying to hush me.

'I'm sorry, I'm sorry, I miss you!' I sing, until I'm standing in front of her, doing prayer hands. The tram stops and I nearly fall over backwards. Vee has curled down into her seat and her ears are red.

'We're sorry. Please, we need your help. And ... **STACKS ON!**' I jump so I'm half-sitting, half-lying on her lap. Jessie jumps on top of me. We're a heavy tangle of arms and schoolbags and laughter.

'Please, please forgive us? And help us,' I beg, into her armpit.

'Fine. Fine. But get OFF me,' Vee says and we scramble to our feet.

Luckily, the person who was sitting next to Vee decides to stand up, so we all squeeze together on the one seat.

'OK,' I whisper. I realise it's going to be very difficult to have a secret meeting now the whole tram is watching us. I huddle in close to my bonus sisters. 'How do we get evidence against Mr Hinkenbushel?'

'We need to watch his door, and then follow him wherever he goes,' Vee says.

I feel my heart relax because she's on our team again.

Jessie nods. 'A stake-out!'

'But we can't watch his apartment door,' I object. The others agree. That would last about three minutes before Alice put a stop to it.

'The street door then,' Jessie says. 'Let's make a list of all the reasons to hang around out the front.'

This is a really good plan, because Jessie likes lists and Vee likes thinking of ways to be **sneaky**.

Jessie gets out her notebook and writes:

Take Baby out for his nap.

We stare at it. Good. But it only lasts for as long as Baby's asleep.

Vee says, 'We offer to run all the shopping errands and then one of us stays behind at the front door.'

Jessie writes it down, but it's the same problem. There's a time limit.

'Pretend we want to play on the footpath because we're not allowed to play in the corridor,' Jessie says.

Straight away, I know it's **genius**. We could do that for hours.

Chapter Eight

Vee 'borrows' footpath chalk from the gym at school and Jessie googles hopscotch, so by the time we get home we're ready to start the stake-out.

I leave Jessie and Vee on the footpath and take the lift up with all our bags. I tell Alice what we're doing and she says, 'Hopscotch! That was **retro** when I was in primary school. Well, don't annoy anyone, and stay away from the road.'

Jessie tells us what to do because she's read the rules. She even demonstrates hopping down the court. It's weird because she doesn't play bunk-bed moves or do rock-climbing or anything sporty usually. I thought hopscotch would be a dumb game for little girls but after we've played it a bit, I start getting really into it. There's a rhythm in the skip of it that's **satisfying**.

We all keep glancing at the front door, but Mr Hinkenbushel doesn't come or go.

I get better at not landing on the lines and Vee is really good at tossing the stone exactly in the square. Jessie isn't as good as either of us, but she does keep playing. It's like, because we have the purpose of the stake-out, she doesn't mind that she's not as good as us.

We do **hopscotch stake-out** after school every day, but nothing happens. Until Friday. We're about to give up and go to the park instead, and finally, Mr Hinkenbushel comes out the front door of our building. He walks straight past our hopscotch game and down the street.

We all stare at each other. I suddenly realise how stupid we've been. We don't even have an excuse to follow him.

'I'm going,' I whisper.

'But –' says Jessie.

'What's the point of the stake-out if we don't follow him?'

'I'm coming too,' says Vee.

'OK then, me too,' says Jessie.

I shake my head. 'We can't *all* go.'

Mr Hinkenbushel is getting smaller and smaller, disappearing down the street.

'Why not?' Vee asks.

After staring at each other for a second, we all turn and run after him.

When we get closer, we tumble to a walk. I hold up my hand for quiet and we all start to tiptoe down the footpath. I dodge along in the shadowy section of a wall and the others follow.

Mr Hinkenbushel looks a bit nervous. He's going at a funny speed. Not quite fast and not quite slow, but kind of twitchy. Nervous. He's pulled a hat down over his eyes and he's **peeking** out from under it like he doesn't want anyone to see his face. He crosses a road and we just manage to make the same lights as him.

On the other side of the road, he seems to see something. Then he slows right down so we're about to catch up with him. Vee pulls my sleeve and pretends to look in a shop window. We line up next to each other, looking in the window, trying not to laugh. It's men's shirts. **Really boring**.

'What's he *doing*?' Vee whispers.

He seems to be dawdling. Then he suddenly picks up his pace. I realise he's following somebody else. I'm pretty sure he's following a tall man with a big gold watch and very shiny shoes, who has just stepped out of a bank. The tall man strides along the footpath. Mr Hinkenbushel **dodges** after him, and we follow in a line behind.

'Who's the new guy?' Jessie whispers from the back.

'No idea,' Vee says.

'Do you think Mr Hinkenbushel is going to do something bad?' I ask over my shoulder.

'Should we call the police?' Vee sounds a bit nervous.

But we don't have a phone and anyway, the police won't believe anything we say now they've seen our revenge video.

They didn't believe anything before they saw it.

Just then the tall man stops.

Mr Hinkenbushel stops behind him, and we stop behind Mr Hinkenbushel.

We're like a set of **dominos** ready to be tipped over.

The tall man has reached into his pocket to answer his phone.

'Good afternoon,' he says, in a voice I recognise straight away.

It's Lord Smiggenbotham-Chancery.

Chapter Nine

At first I'm so **dumbstruck** that I just stand there. Mr Hinkenbushel is following Lord Smiggenbotham-Chancery!

Until this moment, part of me thought I was probably wrong. I was kind of just playing a big game with the diamond smugglers and the stake-out. But now I think it's real. Now I know I was right.

I pull Jessie and Vee over to a tram stop and we lean against the glass, pretending to wait for the tram. Mr Hinkenbushel is very nearby, half in the queue for a coffee cart.

But really, we're all listening as hard as we can to Lord Smiggenbotham-Chancery's phone call.

'This is absolutely our last chance,' he declares into his phone. His posh voice sounds less lazy than usual. 'If we don't make our move tonight ...' Then he pauses. 'If you cannot manage to locate the documentation, then I shall do it alone.' He hangs up and scowls down at his phone. 'Utterly useless,' he mutters.

'He's very angry with the police,' I whisper.

Jessie nods. 'Well, they're not doing a very good job.'

I wonder what Mr Hinkenbushel will do now. He's turned around. His hat is off now and he's almost **strutting**. He actually looks quite pleased with himself, almost as though he *wants* to be seen. We trail behind him but he just goes straight home. Jessie and Vee and I look at each other, confused. Why did he even go out in the first place?

Mr Hinkenbushel stops in front of the door of our building to answer his phone.

Jessie silently passes me the hopscotch stone and I toss it onto the court and start hopping. I don't have to strain my ears to hear what Mr Hinkenbushel has to say.

'I'm out. I'm catching a plane to Sydney

this evening,' he says quite loudly. 'For a meeting, but I'll be back tomorrow.' He pauses. 'Yes, the document is in my apartment, all safe.'

Then he nods, hangs up, and glances down the street. I follow his gaze. Was that Lord Smiggenbotham-Chancery ducking round the corner?

Mr Hinkenbushel looks pleased for some reason and goes inside. Is he pleased because of the phone call? Or did he do something we didn't notice to Lord Smiggenbotham-Chancery?

We wait until the lift doors close.

'The document!' I say. 'It's right there, *next door to our place.*'

Jessie shakes her head. 'He could have been talking about any document.'

'We just caught him following Lord Smiggenbotham-Chancery!' I say. 'Of course it's the document.'

'Are we a hundred per cent sure that was Lord Smiggenbotham-Chancery?' Jessie asks.

'**A million per cent**,' I say.

We all nod. We've heard his voice enough times.

'But they didn't talk to each other,' she says. 'It *could* have been a coincidence that they were in the same place at the same time.'

'But it wasn't,' Vee says.

We all nod. Mr Hinkenbushel deliberately went looking for Lord Smiggenbotham-Chancery, made sure Lord Smiggenbotham-Chancery saw

him, and then walked away. We just don't
know why.

Dinner isn't quite ready so I lie on the
floor with Baby, giving him my finger
to grip and then pulling his little fist
around. But I'm not really paying Baby
any attention. I'm thinking.

Mr Hinkenbushel is going away and
his flat will be empty. The police and Lord
Smiggenbotham-Chancery have no idea
how to find the missing document that
will lead them to the smugglers. And the
document is in Mr Hinkenbushel's flat,
which will be **empty** tonight.

I skype Mum.

She coos at Baby and tries to make him clap but he just wriggles his hands at her. He's not coordinated enough to clap yet. Then he tries to **eat the iPad** so I leave him on the rug and take Mum into our room.

'Mum, those diamond mines. Are they really bad?' I ask.

'Yeah, Squishy.' She nods. 'They're really bad.'

'OK.' She's helping me make a decision, even though she doesn't know it. 'And, Mum, what would you do if the police didn't believe you, but you knew you were right?'

Mum suddenly looks suspicious. 'Is this about that revenge gang thing? Have the police been round again? Do I need to speak with your father?'

I forgot she only **just** found out about the HRC video, and of course she's still worried.

'Mum, it's *fine*, nothing else has happened.'

'Sure?'

'Sure I'm sure.'

'Mum, it's about something totally different …' I make up a little lie. 'It's a thing I'm doing for school … about … um … justice.'

She still looks a bit suspicious, but also thoughtful. 'What was your question? What would I do if the police didn't believe me?' She thinks it over. 'Is it about something important?' she asks.

I nod.

'I suppose …' She's still thinking. 'I suppose I'd do everything I could to **prove** I was right.'

Chapter Ten

It's really late. Dad and Alice have gone to bed and Baby has stopped crying.

It's time.

'Vee,' I whisper. 'Let's do it.'

'Whaa…?' Vee sounds groggy. She must have been asleep.

I feel Jessie sit up. 'You two are **bam-bam crazy**,' she says.

I'm already pulling my pyjamas off. I've got my climbing clothes underneath.

We planned it all after dinner. I get to be the one, even though Vee's been climbing longer than me. I thought she'd argue more, but after she looked down out the window, she went a bit white and let me.

While I tie myself into my makeshift climbing harness, Jessie says all the things she said before we went to bed.

'You'll fall. You'll die. There's nothing there anyway. The police will come and put you in jail.'

Vee anchors the rope around the bedpost and holds it, ready to belay me. My harness is made of climbing rope and a leather belt and it's really strong.

'I won't fall,' I say. 'Vee's got me. Haven't you, Vee?'

Vee nods, biting her lip.

'It's a question of trust, right?' I say. I'm grinning and afraid at the same time.

I open the window. Jessie goes quiet and stands behind Vee to hold the rope.

Then I climb out onto the windowsill. The ground is a really long way down. The tops of the trees are a really long way down. My heart starts **thundering**, my throat blocks up and I feel like my forehead is burning from the fear.

I know my harness is good, and I can feel the strength of Vee's hands on the end of the rope. It's only two metres across to the balcony and the handholds are easier than the easiest wall at the climbing gym. This is nothing.

It doesn't **feel** like nothing.

It feels like the **scariest** thing I have ever, ever done.

But I can't climb back inside now.

I reach along the wall for the first brick and curl my fingers around it. It feels solid. I can do this. I have to trust myself. I nudge my toe out and find a hold.

My fingers feel strong and I know what I'm doing. I **inch spider-ways** across the wall. Trying not to think about the drop. Trying not to think about being an idiot and Jessie being right. Just feeling the gentle tug of the rope that tells me Vee is holding on. I try to focus on the strength in my fingertips.

I reach the balcony rail and swing myself over it onto the tiles. I collapse and just sit there, feeling sick. I already

know that was the stupidest thing I've ever done. You'd think I'd be relieved that I didn't die. But I'm not. Also, I know I have to do the whole thing again to get back.

'You OK?' Jessie hisses from the window.

'Yep,' I say. 'Shhh.'

If Alice and Dad wake up and realise what's happening, they'll probably disown us. Then send us to some horrible boarding school for criminally minded children, or feed us to ravenous sharks. And Mum would fly back from Geneva to help them.

I make myself stand up and unclip the harness. Mr Hinkenbushel's balcony door is exactly the same as Alice and

Dad's, but it opens into a lounge room instead of a bedroom. Lucky, because I do *not* want to see Mr Hinkenbushel's underwear.

I look quickly around his lounge room, which is pretty bare. There's not much here. The first door I try, I can tell this is where I need to look. There are bookshelves with lots of folders on them, and a computer on a desk with a mess of paper everywhere. I think whatever I'm looking for must be very well hidden, so I'm ready to do a thorough search.

But the first thing I see, as though it's been placed there for me to find, is an official-looking piece of paper.

'*The Cantaloupe Diamonds, purchased to the value of …*' I stare at the number printed on the page. The row of zeros seems to blur and I can't count them.

I've found it. The document the police are looking for. It was too easy!

Then I hear a noise that makes my heart jump out of my mouth.

Someone is turning the handle of Mr Hinkenbushel's front door.

Chapter Eleven

I stand there, **gripping** the piece of paper, as a key turns and the lock clicks open. Mr Hinkenbushel is home early. I look around fast. I don't have time to run to the balcony and climb back across. I'll have to find somewhere to hide. Under the desk? What if I just stand really still? I flick off the torch and edge up against the wall. Maybe he won't come into the study.

But he does. It's strange. He doesn't turn on the light. He just walks straight to the study doorway and stands there, a **tall** and **scary** shadow. Actually, he's really tall. Taller than Mr Hinkenbushel. The silhouette looks familiar but it's definitely not our next-door neighbour.

He turns on a torch, and starts to rummage through the papers on the desk. I suddenly realise who it is.

'Lord Smiggenbotham-Chancery!' I say with a wash of relief.

He gives a little **scream** and drops his torch.

'It's just Squishy Taylor,' I say, turning on my own torch, and shining it at him. 'I live next door. I've been trying to catch him too.'

Lord Smiggenbotham-Chancery squints and shades his eyes. 'Trying to catch … who?' he asks.

'Mr Hinkenbushel, the diamond smuggler!' I say. 'And I think I've found what you're looking for. It's the forged receipt, right?' I add, waving the piece of paper.

Lord Smiggenbotham-Chancery picks up his own torch and stares at me strangely. Then he shakes his head. 'Good gracious, yes. Mr Hinkenbushel, the diamond smuggler!' He smiles an odd kind of smile and **snatches** the receipt out of my hands. 'Have you read this?' he asks, looking at me sharply.

'Enough to know it's a receipt for *very* expensive diamonds,' I say.

'But not …' He checks himself and looks it over. 'Ah, yes. This is just the thing. The police will be delighted. I shall just … go now … to the … police station. I'll be sure to let them know what a **good little girl** you are.'

He's backing out of the room.

I hate being called a 'good little girl'. But this might work to my advantage.

'Hey, Mr um, Lord? What do you think about coming next door and telling my parents that I was right and everything's OK. Otherwise I have to do that horrible climb back across to my bedroom. Come on.'

I grab his hand and pull him out the door and down the hall towards our place.

'Well, I'd much rather ... um ... my goodness,' he says.

And suddenly we are both staring Alice in the face.

'**What** is going on?' Alice asks. Our door is wide open and all the lights are on inside. Baby is blinking in her arms.

Behind her, Vee mouths, '**Busted**.'

'Ah ... um ... This very good little girl has been helping me with my police investigations into the diamond-smuggling situation.'

Alice looks down at the tangle of rope that is my climbing harness and her eyes **widen**. She opens her mouth to ask a question.

'So sorry to disturb you in the middle

of the night. I think I'll just pop off now …' Lord Smiggenbotham-Chancery trails off.

'I'm going to need a much better explanation than that,' Alice says to him, like she's talking to one of us.

Just then, the lift **pings** and slides open. It's Mr Hinkenbushel. 'Perfect!' I say to Lord Smiggenbotham-Chancery. 'Now you can arrest him and we can all go back to bed.'

Lord Smiggenbotham-Chancery backs away from us all. 'What? Huh? I can't –' Then he pulls himself up and turns to Mr Hinkenbushel. 'You, sir, are a diamond-smuggling criminal,' he declares.

To my surprise, Mr Hinkenbushel **grins**. 'No,' he says. '*You* are.'

Behind us, the stairwell door opens and a woman comes striding towards us.

'Lord Smiggenbotham-Chancery. You are under arrest for theft, fraud and unsafe work practices.'

Vee, Jessie and I stare at each other in **utter disbelief.**

It's Boring Lady.

She turns Lord Smiggenbotham-Chancery around and handcuffs him.

'Nicely done,' she says to Mr Hinkenbushel, who grins again. It's practically a **high-five.**

Chapter Twelve

'But I … I thought *you* were the diamond smuggler,' I say to Mr Hinkenbushel.

'And I thought *you* were just annoying children.' He looks around at all of us. 'Turns out you're not just annoying. You're nosy, **dangerous** and you almost got yourself killed ruining my trap for Lord Smiggenbotham-Chancery.'

My stomach sinks.

'Goodness gracious,' says Lord Smiggenbotham-Chancery, sounding desperate but still posh, with his nose pressed up against the wall. 'I'm not the criminal you're after, my good man! I'm on your side.'

'Rubbish,' Mr Hinkenbushel growls. 'You've been using your special access to the police to hide your scent. But you **stink** too bad to get away with it forever.'

'My, the police in the colonies are rather **crude**, aren't they?' Lord Smiggenbotham-Chancery sneers, but you can tell his heart isn't in it.

Boring Lady gives him a shake. 'That's enough. Let's get you down to the police station.'

Boring Lady pulls a card from her pocket and hands it to Alice. 'I'll let you get back to sleep. But come by in the morning, and bring the kids. We'll want to question them.'

Mr Hinkenbushel follows Boring Lady, who pushes Lord Smiggenbotham-Chancery down the corridor to the lift.

I can hear him complaining as they walk away. 'Careful of my shirt, it creases easily.'

We are all left standing in the corridor. Alice, Baby, the bonus sisters and me. I'm trying to unobtrusively take off my harness.

Alice looks at the card. 'Chief of Special Secret Undercover Operations,' she says.

Dad **stumbles** out, squinting at the light, and asks, 'What's going on?'

The rest of us look at each other and then burst out laughing. Even Baby.

The next morning, Alice takes us across the road to meet the Chief of Special Secret Undercover Operations. Boring Lady doesn't meet us in her normal office, but takes us to a big room with a shiny wooden table and **chocolate croissants**.

She shakes all our hands. 'Thank you for coming,' she says.

I have so many questions. We've been talking about Mr Hinkenbushel being an **undercover agent** since we woke up. And the fact that the document was in his apartment the whole time.

I start talking before we even sit down. 'But how did you and Mr Hinkenbushel already have the receipt?' I ask.

'Squishy!' Alice says.

But Boring Lady nods. 'Good point. Mr Hinkenbushel took it a few weeks ago, while he was undercover, pretending to be a criminal from a different gang. So the smugglers thought they had been **tricked** by other criminals, not caught by the police.'

'*That's* why you told the news you were still looking for it!' Jessie says. 'To protect Mr Hinkenbushel's disguise.' She pauses. 'But then who broke into Mr Hinkenbushel's apartment the first time?'

Boring Lady smiles. 'You are quick, aren't you? It was the smugglers, trying to get their receipt back. Luckily, I was keeping it safe.'

'I don't get it,' I say. 'You had the

226

document. Wasn't that the evidence you needed?'

'Unfortunately it didn't prove Lord Smiggenbotham-Chancery was the one bringing illegal diamonds into the country. So we used the document as bait, to catch him **red-handed**.'

Jessie realises something. 'So Lord Smiggenbotham-Chancery was *meant* to hear Mr Hinkenbushel say he was going out of town, leaving the document in his apartment.'

Boring Lady grins. 'But you heard him too. So tell me, how *did* you end up in the middle of a special police operation?'

She asks us lots of questions and we all **spill** over ourselves trying to answer them. We tell her about the diamond catalogue and the hopscotch stake-out and the homemade safety harness.

When she finally seems satisfied, I ask, 'Will he have to pay his diamond taxes now?'

'That, plus a big fine. And maybe even prison,' Boring Lady says.

Vee has been shifting in her seat. 'But where are the diamonds?' she asks.

'Ah!' Boring Lady says. 'We got the diamonds first. They're what made us realise there *were* smugglers operating in Melbourne. Follow me.'

She leads us down a long corridor into a lift, down to a basement, through a big cage door with a beeping card swipe, and into a room with lots and lots of safes. It's like something out of a movie.

Every safe has a big dial.

She turns one of the dials this way and then that, and pulls out a silvery suitcase, which she puts on a table.

Inside is a plastic bag full of tiny clear stones. They are a little bit shiny. But they don't even look that special.

'I thought they would be **big** and **sparkly**!' I say.

I think about how stupid it is that stones so small could make someone want to steal and lie and be cruel to people.

'What happens to the diamonds now?' Vee asks.

'Mr Hinkenbushel will return them. They will be given back to the miners to sell and feed their families.'

I'm thinking Mr Hinkenbushel might be a nice man after all. But just then, the cage door beeps and Mr Hinkenbushel comes in. He SCOWlS at us and at the suitcase of diamonds.

He obviously thinks showing them to us is a terrible idea.

'Morning, ma'am,' he says to Boring Lady. 'I'm here to sign these out.'

He puts the diamonds away and closes the suitcase. Then he takes it over to a desk on the other side of the room and starts filling out a form.

Boring Lady grins at us. 'He's a **cranky-pants**,' she whispers. 'But he's good at his job.'

As we're stepping out onto the street, I turn back to Boring Lady. 'If you're the chief, how come you just type at your computer all the time? Why don't you act like a spy?'

'**Squishy!**' Alice says, embarrassed.

Boring Lady waves a 'don't worry about it' hand to Alice, and turns to me. 'I have all my meetings in the big room. Your window looks into my quiet office. No-one's allowed to disturb me there *ever*.' She laughs. 'I guess I would be pretty boring to watch.'

That night, Dad talks to Mum for a long time before I'm allowed to. When he **finally** comes out of his room and hands me the iPad, Mum's smiling but also looks a bit serious.

'Sounds like you'll have to take me rock-climbing when I come home,' she says.

I can tell she's worried by the stuff Dad told her.

'Squishy, I'm glad I taught you to be brave and take risks, but ...' She pauses.

'**But don't die?**' I suggest.

She grins. '**Please don't die.**'

'Don't worry, Mum, I won't.'

I get into bed first. Jessie tucks herself in beneath me, and Vee does a celebratory **Clambereeno** up to her bunk.

I lie on my tummy, staring out at Boring Lady's office. The light is off, but now I know she might just be in another meeting room.

I think about the basement room with the safe and the diamonds. I think about traps and criminals being caught red-handed. By me. I grin into the dark. Weird stuff. I love weird stuff.

The End

For Jimmie and Goldie – and your
ridiculous, brave, loving mama.
– Ailsa

For Tim, the best twin brother I have.
– Ben

and the Vase that Wasn't

Chapter One

I slip off my shoes at the door and swing them by the laces. The foyer of our apartment building is pretty much like an ice-skating rink if your shoes are off. I launch into a **massive skid** to the lift, finishing in a crouch like a surfer.

My bonus sister Vee slides her schoolbag after me and follows, stumbling over as she catches up. Her twin Jessie walks in normally behind us.

I call them my bonus sisters because they were the bonus when I moved in with my dad and their mum.

Mostly they're an awesome bonus. Like now. Vee is lying on the floor laughing and when I try to pull her up, she just **slides** along on her back. It makes me laugh until I'm gasping.

As she finally stands up, the lift slides open.

There's a man inside, shouting into his phone. 'It's gone! It's gone!' he says as he steps out of the lift. 'I've been burgled … Yeah, exactly, or **haunted!**'

His eyes are big and he's got a crazy half-smile on his face. 'It just … disappeared!' he says.

'What disappeared?' Jessie asks,

sounding like a grown-up. She steps up beside us with her schoolbag neatly on her back.

She's the oldest, but only by forty-seven minutes. Vee is staring at the man and I'm trying not to laugh.

'My vase,' the man says into his phone. 'My great-grandmother's Ming Dynasty vase.'

'**Stolen?**' I ask out loud, thinking about when our next-door neighbour was burgled.

'No, *disappeared*,' the man says to me, waving his phone. 'My doors were locked. Nothing else had moved. It was like a **ghost** had been there.'

He sounds weirdly excited. Then he notices his phone and puts it back to his ear. He seems to realise that he's been talking about ghosts to three schoolkids.

'Sorry, I got distracted,' he says into his phone. 'Yes. The police! I should go to the police.' He stumbles through the foyer doors and out into the street.

Jessie swipes her card and presses the lift button, while we watch the man dithering on the footpath.

I giggle and want to keep watching, but Jessie pulls us into the lift.

'I don't know why he didn't just phone the police,' Jessie says.

This is so weird. The cool kind of weird. I do the man's crazy grin and flapping hands and say, 'Haunted!' It comes out half like the man and half like Scooby Doo.

We laugh, collapsing against the lift wall.

'You're hilarious, Squishy,' Jessie says.

That's right. My name is Squishy.

Squishy Taylor. It's like the gangster, Squizzy Taylor, only better.

I love that Jessie said I was **hilarious**. Sometimes she just rolls her eyes when I think I'm funny. Not this time. It makes my laugh even bigger.

We're still laughing when the lift opens at our floor.

Mr Hinkenbushel is standing there, waiting for the lift. He's our next-door neighbour, the **crankiest** man in the universe *and* an undercover policeman. He winces at our noise and scowls at us. We freeze because one of the rules is that we have to be really quiet and not disturb him.

'Well, hurry up and get out of the lift. What are you waiting for? Lousy kids.'

We stumble out past him. I bump him with my bag and he growls.

Seriously. Growls.

And this isn't even that bad. When he shouts, he spits.

When the lift closes, we all breathe out and run down the corridor to our apartment.

Jessie pushes open the door and Alice says, 'Hi, kids,' from where she's typing at the kitchen table. She is working at home because it's Tuesday.

The twins say, 'Hi, Mum.'

I say, 'Hi, Alice.'

Alice and my dad had a Baby, so now we all live together. I used to live with my mum but she got a big job in Geneva and I decided to stay with Dad.

Baby is sitting in the middle of the rug. Jessie's old collection of Barbies is spread out around him. He picks up one without a head and waves her around excitedly. Then she flies out of his hand, but it takes him a moment to realise she's gone.

We all laugh at his surprised face and **swoop** down on him.

'Baby-Baby-Baby,' Vee says in a **gooey growl**, sprawling down onto her stomach beside him and mushing her nose into his big cheek.

I drop my bag and do a commando roll over the couch, stopping just short

of his feet. 'You big, big fatty-boombah,' I say, jiggling his round legs. He's so fat he's got creases at his *ankles*.

Jessie has nuzzled in from the other side and Baby squeals and giggles and flaps his arms around.

'Can we have toast on the balcony?' Jessie asks.

It's a treat, because the balcony door is in Alice and Dad's room, and they keep it for special. We're allowed free rein in the rest of our little apartment, but their bedroom is for them and Baby, and the balcony is grown-ups only.

'Yep, OK. Fine,' Alice says. 'Just don't talk to me for another fifteen minutes.' Her nose is about ten centimetres from her computer screen and she hasn't stopped typing.

'Yay!' Vee says, kicking my bag out of the way and going for the toaster.

'Hey, Alice,' I say, sliding Baby some more Barbies with my foot, 'you should have seen the guy in the foyer –' Jessie and I start giggling.

But Alice doesn't want to know. 'Squishy, I said, don't talk to me.'

Even my **bonus mum** calls me Squishy. My real name is Sita, after my grandma, but people only call me that when I'm in serious trouble.

Vee hasn't given up on our story. 'But the guy in the foyer –'

'Do you want to have your toast on the balcony or not?' Alice asks, actually looking up from her screen.

'Balcony!' we say in unison, and I get out the butter and Vegemite, silent as a **ninja**.

When we work as a team, the three of us are *fast*.

As soon as we're on the balcony, we see Haunted Guy hurrying back up the street with Mr Hinkenbushel beside him.

'I guess Haunted Guy found the police station,' I say, with my mouth full of Vegemite toast.

I lean my elbows on the balcony and look down. My curls get in my mouth with my next bite of toast. I try to **spit** my hair out and the chewed toast goes too. It **tumbles** down through the air, past all the other balconies. I laugh and a few more bits fall out. Luckily they don't hit Mr Hinkenbushel.

Five minutes later, we hear Haunted Guy's voice. He's on the balcony just above us.

Chapter Two

'Yes, *all* the locks!' Haunted Guy says. '*Everything* was locked!' He sounds almost upset, but mostly like I would feel – like he's having an **adventure**.

We hear Mr Hinkenbushel's familiar cranky voice.

'Absurd ... security cameras ... ridiculous to say it just disappeared.'

The talking drops to mutters so we can't hear words anymore.

Jessie whispers, 'What are they saying?'

I don't know. I really want to hear. I put my finger to my lips and climb, as quietly as I can, onto the balcony table. Jessie looks a bit nervous, but I don't care. I stretch my neck, trying to hear.

Haunted Guy's voice is quiet, but I catch a few words. 'No, nothing else moved. Only the vase.'

Then more murmurings.

I feel the table **wobble** and realise Vee is climbing up beside me. She's pointing, showing me the long beams holding the balcony over our heads. If I push up to my **tippiest tiptoes**, I can get my hands halfway around a beam. It's not exactly like monkey bars, but near enough.

Jessie is shaking her head, eyes wide, but Vee offers me a step with both hands. I haul myself up with my biceps, like a chin-up, with Vee's hands helping.

From here, I can hear Haunted Guy better. He's saying, 'I'll have to call my sister. It was Ming Dynasty. Absolutely priceless. Acquired in the Opium Wars ... disappeared ... spirited away. I was only gone one night.'

A door clicks. They've gone inside. Ming Dynasty. Opium Wars. What does it mean? I look down at Jessie, then past Jessie to the street, eleven storeys below.

I suddenly realise how close I am to the edge of the balcony. And that once you're standing on the table, there's no rail to stop you falling. My hands are slippery and shaky and I can't hold on anymore. I **drop, slither, stumble** and **crash** my way back to the floor, quick as I can. I take a moment to stop being scared.

Then I tell the others everything I heard.

We stare at each other.

A priceless vase, disappeared from an apartment where all the doors were locked.

'Cool!' I say.

'**Freaky**,' says Vee.

'We have to google this,' says Jessie.

Then Baby starts crying inside and Alice calls, 'Homework! Now!'

We run into the lounge room and I

do a leapfrog over Vee onto the couch. She falls on top of me, giggling.

'Oops, ow – get off me!' I laugh.

Baby stops crying and does his **cutest chuckles**.

Jessie sets up her homework at the kitchen table and starts working with her head down. Vee and I spread our things out. Then we make up a game where you pretend to jump on Baby and miss just at the last minute. He thinks it's the best thing ever.

Alice starts clattering in the kitchen and Dad walks in wearing his cycling clothes. His legs look so skinny and funny.

'Hello!' He comes round and gives us all **forehead-kisses**.

'Hi, Tom,' Jessie and Vee say, as they get *my* traditional Dad-hello.

I'm not used to them getting the same treatment as me, so I have to go back for more. I jump up on his back while he's cuddling Alice.

'Ooof!' We all stumble into the bench and Alice giggles.

'You're getting a bit heavy for that, Squisho,' Dad says.

I slide down his back, onto the floor. 'Hey, did you know a vase disappeared from the apartment upstairs?'

Dad grins. 'Oh and I suppose Mr Hinkenbushel stole it, hey?'

Dad's joking because every time something goes wrong, I think it's Mr Hinkenbushel's fault.

'Daaaad,' I say, whacking his leg. 'It wasn't Mr Hinkenbushel, it was a burglar. Or a ghost!'

'Ow!' he says. 'You're scarier than a burglar and a ghost combined.'

I hit his leg again for good measure, and he takes Baby to change his nappy and have a shower.

But then I wonder about it. Mr Hinkenbushel is going to be investigating. What will he find?

Chapter Three

After dinner, I sit on the couch and skype Mum in Geneva.

'Hi, Squishy. Hi, Jessie,' she says, waving from her desk.

I didn't realise Jessie was behind me. 'Hi, Devika,' Jessie says, leaning her elbows on the back of the couch.

'What's going on?' Mum asks.

'Well,' Jessie says. 'Squishy gets **shotgun** on the iPad while she's talking to you, but we desperately need to google things.'

Vee leans over my other shoulder. 'So we're here to hurry you up.'

Mum laughs, but I'm a bit annoyed. First they get my special **Dad-forehead-kiss**, then they butt in on my skype with Mum.

'What do you need to google?' Mum asks.

Jessie doesn't even stop to think. 'Ming Dynasty vases and the Opium Wars.'

How does she remember that stuff? She wasn't even the person who heard it first.

'Well,' says Mum, leaning back. 'I can tell you about the Opium Wars.' Of course she can. Mum knows everything about international relations. That's why she works at the UN. 'Basically, the Chinese refused to buy opium from the British, so the British went to war with them.'

'What?' Vee says. 'Why?'

'To force the Chinese to buy opium.'

'But that's crazy!' Vee says.

Mum does her sideways smile and nods. 'Crazy,' she agrees.

'So then,' Jessie says, scooting round to sit next to me, 'what would it mean that a vase was "acquired during the Opium Wars"?'

Mum laughs. 'It means some British pirate stole the vase from its rightful owner.'

'Pirates!' Vee says. 'Awesome!' She makes a hook hand and wrinkles her face. 'Arrrrr!'

Mum laughs even harder. She actually thinks Vee is funny.

'OK, guys,' I say. 'Go away! Let me talk to my mum now.'

'Sorry, sweetie,' Mum says. 'Gotta run.

My next meeting started three minutes ago. Love you, Squishy.'

'Love you,' I say, even though I'm not ready for her to go.

'Bye, kids!' She waves.

'Bye, Devika!' the twins say and then Jessie pushes the hang-up button.

'Awesome,' Jessie says and takes the iPad away.

It makes me so **cranky**. She starts reading out all kinds of boring things about the Opium Wars and the British East India Company, and I am the total opposite of caring. I just wanted to talk to my mum.

On the tram to school, me and my bonus sisters **squash** together on a seat. The two ladies opposite are looking at one phone. It's that stupid YouTube clip of a kid dancing we were all laughing at last week, I can tell from the music. Vee smirks at me.

When it finishes, one of the ladies swipes at the phone. 'Did you see this?'

Her friend takes it off her and reads aloud. '*City apartment haunted by the vengeful ghost of ancient Chinese soldier. Priceless Ming Dynasty vase "stolen by the spirits," says owner.*' They both burst out laughing.

'Can I look?' I ask and lean over, trying to see their phone.

'Um … sure,' one of the ladies says.

'**Squishy!**' Jessie says, elbowing me. I know I'm being rude, but I don't care. The lady is already showing us a picture of a tall white vase, decorated with curving blue pictures of trees and mountains.

The tram **dings** outside school and we pile off together, saying, 'Thanks, bye!' to the ladies.

We start crossing the road and Vee asks, 'Do you think there's really a ghost?'

She looks pale.

Her face reminds me that Vee '**accidentally**' watched a horror movie at a sleepover a few weeks back. It freaked her out so badly that Alice had to come pick her up, even though it was after midnight.

Now she's got that same look on her face, like she just came home from the horror movie.

She grabs my sleeve. 'Maybe a ghost *did* take the vase.'

Vee looks seriously scared. And I know the best thing to do with fear. **Face it head-on**.

'Let's sneak out tonight and try to find the ghost,' I say, pushing open the school gate. It gives me a fun kind of creepy feeling, but Vee turns even whiter. Part of me knows we probably won't see anything, but it would be fun anyway.

Jessie has an even better idea. 'Let's hack into the security footage from the night and *really* see.'

Genius.

That's the thing about Jessie. She can be so boring one minute, and **so** **brilliant** the next.

Chapter Four

Jessie and Vee mostly don't talk to me at school because they're five and a half months older than me. Which is fine – my school friends are better than theirs. My friends and I spend lunch and recess playing monkey-bar tag. If you touch the ground, you're it. I'm **super-ninja** at it since I started rock-climbing and bunk-bed acrobatics. I'm like a monkey god with a hundred arms.

Vee passes just as I'm doing a **kick** up to the top bar. She's talking to her friends from the horror-movie sleepover.

'Really,' she says. 'An actual ghost.'

'Ooooh,' one of them says, sounding impressed. 'Aren't you **terrified?**'

Then I get tagged from behind.

After dinner, I tell the grown-ups that I'm skyping Mum and grab the iPad. Jessie and Vee follow me and we sit on Jessie's bed.

I type: **Love you, Mum, way too much homework, talk tomorrow night?**

She sends a whole row of kisses, which is short for: **I love you, I'm busy too.**

Done.

I'm handing the iPad over to Jessie so she can work her **hacker magic** when another message appears on the screen. Mum has clearly been thinking.

Since when did you do your homework?

We all laugh.

Jessie sends Mum a wink emoji. Then she gets down to work. It's no fun watching Jessie google things. She flicks between windows so fast, you can't actually read anything.

'Ah. Right,' Jessie mutters. 'How do I get into this security footage?' Jessie stops at a screen with some instructions and a password box. 'Hmm. All residents have password access to security footage from their own floor for two weeks. Mmm. After that –'

'Boring!' I say.

Which gives me an idea.

'What do you reckon Boring Lady's doing?' I ask Vee.

We do Desk-Leap-Scrambles up to her bunk and then Rolling-Spin-Drops down to mine. We take it in turns to look at Boring Lady through the telescope.

Her light is still on. Boring Lady is known to some people as the Chief of Special Secret Undercover Operations. But not to us. Our bedroom window looks straight across at her quiet-work room, so all we ever see her do is type. Boring.

We wave to her, but she doesn't look up.

Our telescope is really good. It's supposed to be for looking at stars, so you can see every single one of Boring Lady's eyelashes.

We take it in turns to jump up and down in front of the window, but she doesn't see us.

'Wonder what she's working on?' I say, while Vee looks through the telescope.

'Ha!' Jessie says, from below. 'Equal-seventh most basic password ever! I'm in.'

We drop onto her bunk. The screen is divided into two black-and-white scenes showing the twelfth-floor corridor. It's like two grainy YouTube clips next to each other. One shot is from the lift and the other from the stairwell door. They're both empty.

'The thief must have come in through the balcony,' I say.

'I haven't searched the right time yet, dummy,' Jessie says, sliding the fast-forward bar down the bottom. 'Let's look at when he first found out ... What time do we get home from school?'

Suddenly the screen shows Haunted Guy appearing out of his door, waving his arms and running towards the lift. She slides it some more and then he and Mr Hinkenbushel walk back down the corridor.

'OK, sooo –' Jessie says, sliding the bar back further in time to the night of the haunting.

'There!' Vee and I say at the same time. Jessie freezes the screen.

We all stare at it. For the first time, I **really, truly** believe in ghosts.

It's an olden-days-looking Chinese soldier, standing perfectly still. He's wearing armour carved with **dragons** and a helmet covering his eyes. He's holding a spear. He doesn't move once.

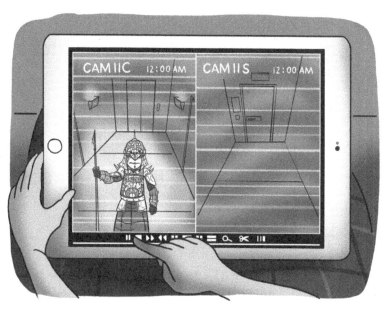

Jessie slides the time-bar forwards and backwards. At 11.59, there's nothing. Then at midnight, the ghost suddenly appears. It stands absolutely still for exactly thirteen seconds. You might not think thirteen seconds is a long time, but when you're looking at a **ghost**, I promise you, it is. After exactly thirteen seconds, it fades to white and then disappears.

'**No way!**' Jessie whispers. 'No way, no way!'

I realise Vee's hand is gripping mine.

Jessie starts sliding the time-bar back and forth, like she'll find something we've missed.

Then the screen freezes.

A text box flashes up and the words

Don't you dare appear in it, one letter at a time. It's like there's a ghost inside the iPad.

Vee gives a little scream.

Then a profile picture loads beside the words. It's Mr Hinkenbushel.

Mr Hinkenbushel is actually writing to us on our screen: **Nosy brats,** he says. **If you do this again, I'll seize your iPad for evidence. Go play hopscotch.** The security screen slides away and we're back to the Google homepage.

Jessie gasps. 'How did he **do** that?'

Vee: 'It was a ghost. Was it a ghost?'

Jessie: 'No, it was Mr Hinkenbushel. He must be tracking who else is accessing the footage as part of his investigation.'

Vee: 'But before that. There was a ghost before that.'

I'm a little bit scared of the ghost. I'm more worried about Mr Hinkenbushel. I don't want him to be in our iPad. I don't want him to SPY on us. The iPad is the only way for me to talk to Mum. It makes me kind of angry, thinking Mr Hinkenbushel could look at me talking to her.

'Can Mr Hinkenbushel see what we're doing on the iPad whenever he wants?' I ask.

Jessie frowns. 'No. Why would you think that?'

'Because he was just there, talking to us.'

'I think,' Jessie explains, 'he can only

talk to us from the security website. Maybe because he's investigating, he can see what anyone on that website is doing.' She pauses and shakes her head. 'He can't just look at us anytime. That would be illegal.'

'Oh.' I feel a big wash of relief.

Vee looks half-scared, half-angry. 'I can't believe *that's* what you're talking about,' she hisses. 'Don't you even care that we saw a ghost?'

Chapter Five

Alice sends us off to bed, and we go quietly. The image of that ghost is appearing and disappearing in my mind.

'If the ghost can steal a vase,' Vee whispers in the dark, 'what else can it do?'

'It can't really be a ghost,' Jessie says. 'It's got to be some kind of **hoax**.'

'It could be either,' I say. Whichever way, it's a mystery, so I'm happy.

In the night, I wake up because Vee is climbing out of bed. I get a **fright** and lie there, clutching my blanket. A few moments later, Alice brings Vee back and tucks her in.

'Don't be scared,' Alice whispers. 'I'm here.' She stands for a while next to Vee's pillow. My heart slows back down to normal and I fall asleep before Alice leaves.

Jessie looks extra-thoughtful over breakfast, but doesn't say much. Vee is turning her porridge over without putting any in her mouth. Baby **smashes** bits of apple against the table and drops them on the floor. He's not scared of anything.

We don't talk about the vase, but the whole day I'm a little bit tingly because I know there's something big happening.

'Hey, you guys,' Dad says, as we all arrive home from school. 'Someone got an email from Geneva today.'

'Woohooo!' I shout and run over. Emails from Mum usually mean movie vouchers or music credit.

He shakes his finger, grinning. 'Not for you, Squisho, for somebody else.'

He passes the iPad over to Jessie.

I just stare. *Mum* emailed *Jessie*? The world feels wrong. I can feel my eyes prickling hot and I don't know what to do. Then Dad gives everyone his matching, exactly equal **forehead-kisses**. And I'm suddenly hot-hot angry.

That's **my** dad and **my** mum. It's fine that they live apart. I got used to that ages ago. It's fine that I have to share a bedroom with my bonus sisters. They are actually mostly pretty fun. But I need *some* special things, some things only for me.

I whack the butter knife down on the bench, nearly break the Vegemite jar, and slam the cupboard closed. No-one notices.

Dad asks Vee how school was, looking all concerned because she's so quiet. While Jessie sits at the table, reading an email from *my* mum.

No-one notices me **banging** plates.

'Wow!' says Jessie. She keeps reading silently. Then she says, 'Oh, *what*?'

There's another pause. What does she think we're going to do? Beg to be told what she's reading?

'No way!' Jessie says.

I actually hate her.

'What is it? What does it say?' Vee asks, falling for Jessie's game.

'So …' Jessie says, sounding all smug. 'Devika sent me an article about the Opium Wars. It says there were forty-seven matching vases in a temple, and a British admiral killed the priests and stole all the vases.'

'**Whoa**,' Vee says, pulling her chair closer. 'He killed the priests?'

Jessie nods. 'Later, he sold the vases for lots of money all around the world.'

I'm listening, even though I wish I wasn't. Even though I wish Mum had sent the email to me, not Jessie. I can't help feeling a bit interested.

'Now there's an international treaty,' says Jessie, 'between heaps of museums, agreeing to give the vases back. But they haven't found them all. They think greedy people are keeping them a secret.'

Dad grins. 'This is totally Devika's thing. She loves a bit of righting old wrongs.'

He's right. Mum calls it 'justice work' and it's what she loves about her job.

Then Jessie squeals, which wakes up Baby, who starts howling.

'What?' Dad and I ask.

'It's the same vase,' Jessie says. 'The one from upstairs is one of the forty-seven.'

I run across to look over her shoulder. Dad and Vee crowd in. Jessie shows us the picture from Mum's article. It's exactly the same as the picture we saw on the tram.

Jessie does a search for the news article then flicks between the two pictures.

'So. The vase upstairs was stolen from a temple by a greedy British admiral,' I say.

Vee looks grim. 'And then stolen back by a ghost,' she says.

'What ghost?' Dad asks.

Just then, there's a knock on the door. I run to answer it, because I'm the nearest.

It's Mr Hinkenbushel.

'I need to talk to you, Mr Taylor,' he says, as if I'm not standing right in front of him. 'Your kids have been **hacking** the damn security footage.'

Chapter Six

Dad has gone over to Mr Hinkenbushel's place with Baby. Which feels really weird because Dad and Mr Hinkenbushel don't like each other. But sometimes even adults who hate each other become **allies**, just to gang up on kids.

We're left sitting on the lounge-room floor, waiting to find out what kind of trouble we're in. It's supposed to be dinnertime and no-one's cooking.

Vee looks pretty worried. 'Killing and stealing,' she says. 'That's exactly what makes a ghost.' She's **jiggling** her knee nervously.

'It has to be a hoax,' Jessie says. 'So someone could steal that vase.'

'How *could* it be a hoax?' Vee asks, her voice a bit high.

'Someone in a costume?' suggests Jessie.

'But what about how it just *faded*?'

Jessie shrugs. Vee looks even more creeped out.

I'm creeped out too, but in a good way. **Is it a hoax or haunting?** Either way, it's huge.

'Well,' I say, 'the main thing is that the vase should be returned to China.'

The others nod.

Then I think of something else. 'Why do you think Mr Hinkenbushel wanted to stop us looking at the ghost?'

'It wasn't a ghost,' Jessie says.

'How do you **know?**' Vee asks. It's getting darker outside, and she's looking more and more nervous. There's something a bit catching about the way she jumps and stares around whenever there's a noise.

'I don't know,' Jessie says. 'Let's look at the footage again now, while Mr Hinkenbushel is distracted with Tom.' She's already hunting around for something.

'Dad took the iPad,' I say. I saw him slip it under his arm on his way out.

Jessie stands still, like she doesn't know what do to next.

We need a plan. Vee is **jiggling** like a crazy person and biting her lip.

'In the movie, they did this thing to scare off the ghost,' Vee says. 'They did chanting and drew a magic circle. One man held a big black book.'

It sounds exciting, like a **scary kind of fun**. But Jessie is shaking her head. I can tell she's worried about how seriously Vee is taking the ghost thing.

'We need to look at that security footage again somehow,' Jessie says. 'Or get someone else to.'

'What about Boring Lady?' I suggest.

'What about her?' Jessie asks.

'Well, she *is* the Chief of Special Secret Undercover Operations,' I say.

Vee looks hopeful. 'Do you reckon we could signal her?'

I scramble off the floor and grab the torch from under the sink. I switch it on and **blind** myself. It's definitely bright enough.

We all run into our bedroom.

'Is she there?' Vee asks.

She's there.

I shine the torch towards the window, but it just reflects back at our faces. Jessie takes the torch and pushes it against the glass. She scrapes it from side to side.

I do a **high kick** up to my bunk and sprawl, staring through the telescope and thinking, *Look at us, Boring Lady,* *look at us.* But she doesn't. She just keeps typing. Her face is **concentratey** – with a little frown.

Vee is getting more desperate. 'This isn't working.'

'OK, what about this?' Jessie runs to the door and switches our bedroom light on and off, on and off. Surely Boring Lady will notice a whole window flickering.

She doesn't.

'Boring Lady, help!' Vee shouts. Even though we all know she can't hear us.

'We could email her,' Jessie begins, then stops herself. 'Only we don't have the iPad.'

It's starting to feel like Dad and Alice are never coming home and Vee looks **panicky**.

'OK, you know what we should do?' I say. 'You know who *would* believe us?'

The others look at me.

'Haunted Guy!' I say. 'Maybe he'd let us look at the ghost on *his* computer.'

We stare at each other for a moment.

Vee says, 'You're right. If anyone believes us, he will.'

'Should we go visit him?' I ask. 'Now?'

That's when Dad walks in with Baby. And he is **mad**.

We eat cheese on toast for dinner in silence while Alice puts Baby to bed and Dad skypes Mum. He talks to her for ages in our bedroom – probably all about how **bad** I am. When he comes back with Mum still on the iPad, it should be my turn.

But it's not. Dad props Mum up on the kitchen table and makes us sit where we can see her.

'Family meeting,' he says, as Alice steps in quietly, closing the door.

I groan. 'Family meeting' translates to: 'Adults talk too much. Kids get bored.' I just want to visit Haunted Guy.

The adults take it in turns to tell us about using the internet responsibly. Which is exactly as interesting as I guessed.

'From now on, we're going to have a new rule,' Alice says. 'You're only allowed to use the iPad in the lounge room.'

Jessie protests.

I look at Mum, who's looking seriously out of the screen. 'But what about when I skype you?' I ask.

She shakes her head. 'Sorry, Squisho. Lounge room only. You just lost your privileges.'

We do pleading faces. We promise

to be **so, so, so good**. The grown-ups don't shift.

Then I have to hang up on my mum without talking to her properly. Again. That's the third night in a row that we haven't talked properly.

And it's too late to go visit Haunted Guy. They make us go straight to bed. We're not even tired.

Vee actually climbs the ladder to her bunk. I don't think I've ever seen her do that. Alice flicks off the light and I hear Vee's breathing get frightened.

I don't care. At least her mum kisses her goodnight. I'm not even allowed to talk to my mum.

Chapter Seven

I wake up in the dark with something touching my face.

'Can you hear that?' Vee whispers. She's hanging over the side of the bunk. Her fingers are tapping my ear.

I scrabble at her hand. '**No, shhh**,' I say.

I listen for a while, but don't hear anything.

'We need to do that thing they did in

the movie to scare off the ghost,' Vee says, sounding scared.

'Vee, go back to sleep.'

In the morning, Vee looks ragged. Over breakfast, she talks to Dad and Alice about hauntings in a scared voice. They are too rushed to really notice. But this ghost thing is getting serious.

'Let's go straight to Haunted Guy's after school and get this straight,' Jessie says in my ear as the tram **dings** through the rain. She's looking at Vee's tired face.

I nod. I want to discover the truth *and* look after Vee. We're on a mission.

Haunted Guy lives on level twelve, which is the very top of our building (apart from the roof). The corridors are exactly the same. His door is almost like ours – only without the **dirty** fingerprints.

'What are we gonna say?' whispers Vee, as Jessie holds out her fist to knock.

'We'll tell him the truth,' Jessie says, hitching up her schoolbag.

'What truth?' I ask, but she's already rapped twice.

Haunted Guy doesn't answer the door. A lady does. She's wearing jeans and a massive bright scarf.

We all smile at her.

'Hello,' she says, smiling back. 'What can I do for you people?'

Grown-ups love it when kids make eye contact, as long as you're smiling. That's something Mum taught me. Even if you feel shy, meet the grown-up's eyes. Gets 'em every time.

'Um … we came to talk to, um … the man who lives here about his … his … missing vase,' Jessie says.

The lady chuckles. 'You mean you want to know all about the **ghost?**' she asks. 'How did *you* hear about it?'

We all talk at once.

Jessie says, 'We live downstairs.'

'We saw him in the foyer *right* after it happened,' I say.

'The ghost was on our iPad, but we're

not allowed to look at it anymore,' Vee explains.

'All right, all right, s|ow down,' the lady laughs. 'Sounds like we're neighbours. I'm Mina, and the man you saw was my brother, Harry. Wanna come in? Harry's still at work, but you can talk to me.'

The apartment is the same shape as ours, but has about one-tenth of the stuff in it.

'Firstly,' Mina says, shoving a laptop aside and piling crackers on a plate, 'the ghost is not real, I promise you. Now sit down.'

We all sit around Harry's table.

Vee says, 'The ghost *is* real, we saw the security footage.'

'You saw the security footage?' Mina looks a little bit surprised and glances at the laptop on the table. Then she looks back at us with arched eyebrows. 'How did you manage that?' Her listening smile reminds me of Mum when I've come home from some crazy adventure.

So Jessie explains about hacking into the security footage and seeing the Chinese ghost. Vee tells about Mr Hinkenbushel stopping us from looking, and how we're banned from the iPad.

I say, 'So Vee thinks it's a ghost and Jessie thinks it's a hoax to steal the vase. Either way, we know the vase needs to be returned to China. We knew if anyone would care about what we discovered, your brother –'

'Harry,' Mina says.

'– Harry would care. And –'

Jessie interrupts. 'And maybe he'd let us check the security footage again on his computer.' She nods towards the laptop.

Mina bursts out laughing. 'You are some seriously **cheeky** kids!' she says. 'Listen, I don't have the password for his computer, so we can't check that security footage. But I promise there's no ghost. OK?'

Vee nods. But I'm annoyed. Even though Mina is funny and nice, we saw the ghost with our own eyes. She doesn't seem to care about the temple at all. She's just making promises with that **grown-up bossiness**, like we should just believe her. Plus, the laptop is **right there** in front of us. I bet Jessie could **crack** the password.

Mina is still talking. 'There's no way that vase is anything special. I keep telling Harry that Mum bought it from a two-dollar shop on Sydney Road, but he's got this whole other story.'

'Ming Dynasty, acquired during the Opium Wars.' Jessie nods, sounding like a teacher.

Mina looks a bit surprised. People don't expect kids to be as smart as Jessie is. 'That's what Harry says, yes.'

'But the police must have looked at the security footage too,' Jessie insists. 'What does Mr Hinkenbushel say?'

'Um … the police couldn't really … help,' Mina says.

Mina looks **weirded out** that we know about Mr Hinkenbushel, so I explain. 'He's our next-door neighbour. We hate him so much that we made a **revenge** video about him one time.'

Mina laughs again. 'You're filmmakers too, huh? I edit video, documentaries mostly.' She reaches for the laptop on the table and then changes her mind. She stands up instead. 'All right. Enough. Don't you kids have somewhere to be?'

She closes the door behind us and we head down to the lift.

'How can she *know* there's no ghost?' Vee asks, sounding hopeful and nervous at the same time.

'She can't know,' I say. I love the mystery of it. **Haunting or hoax?**

'I bet Mina was looking at the ghost too. Bet she wants to make a famous documentary about it.'

'If we could just get on the internet,' Jessie says. 'I bet there's something dodgy in the footage.'

The lift isn't coming.

'Stairs?' I suggest, and we turn and **pelt** for the stairwell, schoolbags bouncing on our backs. When we reach the landing, I look up at the last set of stairs before we go down. These stairs are special, because they go to the roof. They're more like a metal ladder, and they've got a tall gate in the middle to stop people going all the way up.

Stuff designed to stop people is **awesome**, because it's difficult.

Difficult equals fun. Vee and I glance at each other, then ditch our bags and race up the metal ladder together. Our shoulders bump and our arms tangle on the rails, but Vee beats me to the gate.

'Guys,' Jessie calls from below, 'what are you *doing*?'

Vee swings a leg over the gate, then drops down the other side. **Too easy**. I follow and by the time I'm over, Vee is at the very top landing, by the door. You can tell it goes to the outside, because drops of rain are beating underneath. Also, there's a sign on the door saying **Rooftop Access**. It's locked, of course.

Chapter Eight

'I reckon the roof door has the same lock as our balcony,' I say, leaping down the stairs two at a time. 'The **bobby-pin trick** would work for sure.'

Vee laughs. 'Let's do it!'

Jessie shakes her head at us.

When we reach our corridor Mr Hinkenbushel is arriving home, pulling his keys out of his pocket. We stop talking as soon as we see him and he ignores us.

I realise he is the only other person, apart from Haunted Harry, who we *know* has seen the ghost. He was *there*, on the same screen as us.

My heart is all fast and brave from climbing the gate and thinking about the locked door to the roof. I don't stop to think.

'Um, excuse me, Mr Hinkenbushel –'

He turns and glares at me. 'What do you want?'

'Um, what are you doing about that ghost?'

'What?' He looks at me like I'm a piece of dirt.

I don't feel quite so brave anymore, but I keep talking. 'The ghost in the footage. We know you saw it too.'

His face goes red and angry. 'I didn't see a ghost, because there was no ghost.' He gets louder and redder and the **spit** starts to gather around the corners of his mouth. 'You kids think you're *so* clever, but you're just nosy, brainless idiots with nothing better to do than –'

'OK, fine, sorry,' I say.

We **dash** through our own door while he's still shouting.

'Subtle move, Squishy Taylor,' Jessie says and we all laugh.

When I skype Mum in the lounge room, everyone wants to talk to her. Alice comes over with a basket of laundry and starts asking about the Greek economy. Of course Mum won't shut up. Alice stays until every sock is paired. I even help, so she'll go away faster. Mum doesn't notice.

Finally, when Alice leaves, Jessie brings Baby over and lets him **bash** the iPad. Mum just laughs at how cute he is.

Then she has to go. 'Love you, Squishy-sweet,' she says, blowing me a kiss.

It makes me want to cry when she hangs up.

Geneva feels like it's on Pluto, rather than just a plane ride away.

I'm still cranky about missing out on Mum-time when it gets to goodnights. I hardly notice how quiet Vee is. But I do notice when she takes the torch up to bed.

I ask, 'What's that for?'

'Nothing,' she mutters. 'Just so I can see stuff if I need to.'

Dad does his new round of **equal forehead-kisses**, but I duck my head away at the last minute.

'What's up, **Squisho?**'

'Nothing,' I mutter, just like Vee muttered to me. I want him reach in and give me a proper cuddle. But he just leaves.

I can't sleep because I'm cranky about sharing my mum and dad. I think about Mum laughing with Jessie about Baby. I squeeze my eyes closed. I try to think about the vase mystery instead, but it's not fun. **It's just scary**. I roll over and pull my blankets tighter.

I wake up to a light **darting** around the room. It takes me a moment to realise it's Vee with the torch. What's she doing?

She flicks it off after a minute and I lie in the dark.

The bunk ladder starts **creaking** and our bedroom door eases open. Vee is **sneaking** out.

I'm thinking about following her when she comes back in. Dad, stumbling and sleepy, is with her. He stands by our bed, saying, 'It's four in the morning, sweetie. There are no ghosts. Just go back to sleep.'

He's using his special Dad-voice. **My** Dad-voice. It makes me remember all the things I was mad about when I fell asleep.

After he leaves, I can't hold it in anymore.

'He's not your dad, you know,' I say.

'Wha-at?' Vee asks.

'You think you can have my dad? Well, you can't, he's mine.'

Jessie rolls over in the bunk underneath mine. 'What are you guys talking about?' she says sleepily.

Vee says, 'I just had a bad dream.'

She sounds like a whingey little kid. Which is annoying.

'All I'm saying is, he's my dad, not yours,' I say.

'Squishy!' Jessie says. 'Don't be so selfish. She's just freaked out –'

'Me? Selfish? You're the selfish one! You stole all my Mum-time tonight and didn't even *think* about what you were doing.'

'**Whoa**! Squishy, it's the middle of the night and you're being a weirdo,' Jessie says.

I don't say anything.

Then I say, 'I'm not talking to you guys.' Just in case they don't understand the silence.

I realise Vee is crying. Sometimes I'm so much more mature than she is.

'Vee?' Jessie says. 'What's up?'

Vee takes a **sobby** little breath. 'It's the ghost. I can't sleep because of it.'

'There is no ghost,' Jessie says.

'But we **saw** it,' Vee insists.

'We saw a *video*,' Jessie says. 'It could have been anything.'

Vee keeps crying. Even though it's annoying, I can't help feeling a bit sorry for her. I'm so angry and **twitchy**, my bones are **itching** to do *something*.

'Maybe we *should* try to scare off the ghost,' I say, because there's something **scary-exciting** about the idea.

Jessie is silent.

'Jessie?' Vee asks.

'OK, fine,' Jessie says. 'There's no ghost. But we can do it if you really want.'

'Can we do it now?' Vee asks. 'I can't sleep.'

'All right,' Jessie says. 'Where?'

I know exactly where.

'We have to make sure we clear out the **whole building**,' I say. 'That means we have to go up on the roof.'

Chapter Nine

We tiptoe around the dark kitchen with the torch, looking for good things to take. Jessie finds a bobby pin and Vee gets our oldest recipe book, the brown one with gold writing on the front.

'This one's just like the big book in the movie,' she whispers.

I pull open the spice drawer, because there was turmeric and holy basil at my grandmother's funeral. I know funerals are different from **ceremonies** to scare away ghosts, but they're both for saying goodbye to dead people. I want to take candles and the lighter, even though we're not usually allowed, but Jessie makes me put them back. **She's so bossy.**

Jessie slides everything into a green bag, and then spots the iPad. She grabs it too and I take the key off the hook by the door.

We tiptoe out into the dimly lit corridor, and down to the bright stairwell. We run up to the ladder.

I climb the gate easily and Vee follows. Jessie reaches up to pass the bag to me. She starts climbing, but stops with one leg over the top.

'I'm stuck,' she says. She's clutching on, and doesn't want to lift her second leg over the top.

'Come on,' Vee says. 'Just hold tight and lift your foot over.'

Jessie's knuckles are white. She's almost lying along the top of the gate and the foot near me keeps trying to find a new spot. She looks like she doesn't trust herself to put it down.

I remember how scared I was looking down from our balcony, how **shaky** and **slippery** my hands felt.

'You're OK,' I say. I step up under her. 'Tread on me.'

I guide her foot and hold it steady on my shoulder.

'Uh,' she says. 'Is that OK?'

She's kind of heavy, and her foot is **mashing** my ear.

'It's fine,' I say. 'Just a bit squishy.'

Jessie half-laughs, half grunts, then she's over the top and climbing down the other side. Her foot **catches my curls** and yanks at them.

'Ow!'

'Sorry!'

We stand, breathless, by the **Rooftop Access** sign.

'You better be able to pick that lock,' Jessie says.

But, just like I thought, the lock is the same as the one on our balcony. All it takes is just the right **jiggle**, and I'm done. Awesome. I push the door and it swings open.

We're out on the roof. It's wide with a wall all around the edge. The main thing I notice is the city, out beyond the wall. It's huge and sparkling all around.

'**Eeee!**' squeals Vee, running out across the clear space and spinning in a circle.

It's stopped raining and the air is cold

and clear. I can hear the sound of cars below, but so far away.

Behind us, the door we came out of looks like the entry to a little shed.

It's the perfect place.

Vee **scatters** a circle with the basil and places the recipe book perfectly in the middle. I mark our foreheads with turmeric, **swiping up** with my finger like they did at my grandma's funeral.

Jessie hunches over the iPad.

'What are you doing?' I ask, leaning over her shoulder.

'Getting the footage of the ghost,' she says. 'Hang on ... it's pretty low on battery ... but ... here we go.'

The ghost is still there, standing tall and still on the screen. We all stare at it as it fades to white and disappears into an empty corridor.

Then Jessie touches the screen. 'I'll put it on loop,' she says. We watch, **mesmerised**, as the ghost appears and disappears. Jessie places it beside the recipe book in the middle of the circle.

'Hands on the book,' Vee says, as we sit cross-legged around it. We place our fingers on the cover.

Vee looks up and says, 'Now we need to chant.'

'Chant what?' Jessie asks, looking a bit embarrassed.

I think about the *Om Namah Shivaya* chant my grandmother used to do, but that doesn't seem right.

'What about, **go away ghost**?' Vee asks.

But I shake my head. 'We don't just want it to go away,' I say. 'We want justice. We want to return the vase to the temple.'

Then Jessie gets inspired. She's the one who knows good words. 'Ghost be gone and justice will follow.'

Vee grins and I say, 'Perfect.'

So we all chant together:

'Ghost be gone and justice will follow.

'Ghost be gone and justice will follow.

'Ghost be gone and justice will follow.'

We sway around the recipe book with

the screen light shining up on our faces. Jessie is looking down at the iPad, and Vee and I are looking out into the darkness. My voice sounds different and special when it's exactly in time with the others. The night feels **enormous**, spreading out from the roof. Our voices get louder and louder until it feels like something big will happen. The wind blows our hair, smelling of dried basil. We slowly stop chanting.

Everything feels quiet and good.

'Do you think it worked?' Vee asks.

I nod. I think it must have.

Jessie is still focused on the iPad. 'Hey,' she says, snatching it up. 'It **was** a hoax! Look – the video's been edited.'

She points her finger to the screen, at

the doorframe behind the ghost. The frame jumps sideways when the ghost appears, and the shadows get darker in a flash. It jumps back again when the ghost disappears.

'Someone pasted video over the top here,' Jessie says. We stare as it loops again and the doorframe jumps.

'So there was no ghost?' Vee asks.

'No ghost,' I say. I'm actually disappointed.

'But there was *someone* who edited video and stole a vase,' Jessie says, as if to make me feel better.

The iPad's battery is showing 2% charge. I watch the loop flip through again. There's still a mystery to solve.

Then, out of nowhere: BANG!

The door at the top of the stairs slams shut.

Vee screams and we all scramble to our feet and run for the little shed.

There's no handle on the door. Nothing to pull on. Just a keyhole. We scrabble down the side, trying to squeeze our fingers in the tiny gap.

No use.

We're stuck here on the roof.

Chapter Ten

'Help! Help!' Vee shouts as we all run to the edge of the building. The wall is concrete and comes up to my chest. I have to stand on tiptoe to see the street properly. The few tiny people under the streetlights don't look up. Anyway, if they did, they wouldn't see us up here in the dark.

'Do you think the ghost locked us up here?' Vee asks.

'No!' Jessie says. 'There is no ghost, remember? Someone edited the video.'

For the first time, I feel a little bit scared. I glance at the closed door. 'Do you think the person who made the video locked us up here?' I ask.

'No!' Jessie says. 'It was the wind and our own stupid fault.'

I think she's probably right. But we *are* stuck on a roof in the dark. So it's a bit scary anyway.

In a big rush, all I want is Mum. And the iPad is right here. I grab it.

'Good plan,' Jessie says. 'Message Mum.'

But I'm not messaging Alice. I tap through to Skype.

Bloobleep bloobleep.

'Squishy, no,' Jessie says.

But it's already connecting.

Mum's face comes up. She's not at her desk. She's at home with wet hair and a dressing gown.

For one second she squints at me, **confused**.

Then the iPad goes black with a little white turning circle in the centre. It's run out of battery.

'You idiot, Squishy,' Jessie says. 'Skype takes so much more power.'

We watch the last light on the screen fade. This is it. We're really alone up here. For some reason, the black screen reminds me of Dad not cuddling me goodnight. I bite my lip and my eyes blur from tears. Both my parents have **deserted** me.

Jessie is frowning. 'We need to get a message to someone.'

She tries to turn on the iPad again, but the battery is definitely flat. Vee rips pages out of the recipe book and runs to the edge and starts folding a paper aeroplane. She throws it down to try and get someone's attention, but it just **death-spirals** into the darkness.

I watch it go and think it needs a message. I try to write **Help** on the next one with wet turmeric instead of a pen, but it ends up a big yellow mess. Jessie stands beside me, flashing the torch towards the street, but nobody notices.

Finally we slide down with our backs against the wall. I'm out of ideas and this has stopped being a fun adventure.

It feels like we're going to be here for the rest of our lives. I'm getting cold. I realise I don't even care about the vase. I just want to go home and eat breakfast.

Vee shivers, and says, 'I'm hungry.'

I realise I can see her face. 'It's starting to get light,' I say. The sky is turning pale all across the horizon.

'We have to figure a way out,' Jessie says. 'Mum and Tom will wake up soon.'

I pull back up to my feet and lean my elbows on the wall, looking across the street. The angles of the buildings and the trees below look very familiar.

'Is that Boring Lady's office?' Vee asks, joining me and pointing.

She's right, it is. And Boring Lady is already at work. She must start early. She's directly across from us, and two floors below. Which means –

'That must be **Haunted Harry's** balcony just down there,' Jessie says.

We're looking straight down at a balcony with a table and some pot plants.

And a big white vase with blue decorations.

Chapter Eleven

Vee stares down at the vase. 'We brought it back. We did it.'

'Vee!' Jessie's got her grown-up voice on. 'There **was no ghost**.'

'Anyway,' I say, 'we haven't finished the job yet. The vase needs to go to that temple in China.'

We all lean out, looking down at the vase glowing white in the orange sunrise. Along the wall are the remnants of us trying to signal our way out: the torn recipe book, the torch, the turmeric.

'We can't do **anything** while we're stuck here,' Jessie says. She starts waving the torch towards Boring Lady. But it's not going to work. Boring Lady never answers our signals.

'We're going to have to climb down to Haunted Harry's balcony,' Vee says.

Jessie is horrified. 'That's insane!'

It's actually not. From Haunted Harry's balcony to here is nowhere near as high as our rock-climbing walls. I can see some good handholds in the stone. If you fell you'd **only fall** as far as the balcony.

'It'll be easy,' Vee says, jutting her chin. 'I'm going to save us.'

'Vee, don't be crazy,' Jessie says, pulling her arm back.

Squishy Taylor to the rescue. I put my palms on the wall and jump, pushing down until my arms are straight. My tummy is bent over the wall. I lift one leg to swing it over.

Jessie shouts, 'No, Squishy, stop it!' and grabs my leg.

That's when I **knock** the jar of turmeric.

It drops down the side of the building, **ricochets** off Haunted Harry's balcony rail and keeps falling. The lid flies off and the powder glides out in a great, spiralling, yellow cloud. The cloud gets bigger and bigger as it drops towards the ground.

And now, finally, Boring Lady has noticed us. She stands at her window, staring first at the cloud and then up at us. I wave wildly, clinging to the wall with my knees, and Boring Lady runs for her phone. She's waving us back with crazy, flinging hands, as if she could push us away from the edge of the wall.

'Hey! What are you kids doing?' It's Haunted Harry. He's staring up at us from his balcony in his pyjamas. He must have heard the jar of turmeric hit the rail.

'We're stuck!' Vee yells.

'We can't get down!' I shout.

'Well, for the love of little fishes, do NOT try to climb down!' he hollers back up at us.

Mina appears beside him and stares up at us, before running back inside.

'Wait right there!' Haunted Harry yells.

So we wait.

The first person to run out the door is Dad. He ignores my bonus sisters and pulls me up into the biggest hug ever.

'We woke up and you were gone,' he says with a mouthful of my hair. 'I was so worried.' He squeezes me really tight.

That's when I know I will **always** belong to my dad, however many bonus sisters I have.

Alice is beside us **cuddling** Jessie and Vee.

Haunted Harry, Mina and Boring Lady are right behind her. We all stand on the roof, laughing and talking. Dad doesn't let me go for a long, long time. Even when he stops hugging me, he keeps hold of my hand.

'How did you find us?' I ask. 'Did Boring Lady call you first, or Haunted Harry?'

'They both got to us pretty quickly,' Dad says. 'But you know who called me first?'

I look at him, not sure.

'Your mum,' he says.

I smile. Now I really, truly don't feel deserted.

'The vase,' I say remembering why we're there. 'It came back!' I try to drag

Dad over to look but he doesn't move, and Alice holds up her hand. 'Wait a second, Squishy Taylor. First things first. What in heaven's name are you three doing up here?'

I don't even know where to start. Vee garbles out the story of the way we got rid of the ghost. Jessie makes sure everyone knows she never believed in the ghost. I interrupt to explain to Mina about being banned from talking to my mum (which Alice tries to explain isn't exactly true). We all tell Boring Lady how many times we tried to signal her. She's the only one in daytime clothes, so it's a raucous rooftop **pyjama party**. The grown-ups are rolling with laughter one minute, and **intrigued** the next.

'But we still don't know who edited the security footage?' Alice asks.

'*That's* what I want to know,' Jessie says. 'It must have been someone who had access to the footage and wanted the vase.'

I'm struck by something. 'But we know somebody who had access to the footage, and r**eally** didn't want us to look at the video,' I say.

They wait for me to answer. 'Mr Hinkenbushel!' I announce.

'Squishy!' Jessie laughs. 'We **know** Mr Hinkenbushel isn't the bad guy.'

Mina coughs, looking embarrassed. 'Actually,' she says, 'it was me. I secretly took the vase to be valued, because I *knew* Harry was wrong. In the meantime

I thought he'd quite like to be haunted –'

Harry grins. '**Loved it**,' he says. 'And so, clearly, did these guys.'

'We sorted it all out with the police on the first day,' Mina explains. 'I had no idea there was a whole other **adventure** going on until yesterday,' she says to the grown-ups. Then she grins at us. 'I'll never try to keep a secret from you guys again.'

I can't tell if I'm disappointed that there's no ghost, or pleased to be friends with a hacker. I can tell which one Jessie is. She's already got a **billion questions** for Mina on the tip of her tongue. But there are more important things than that.

'And now,' I say, turning to Boring

Lady, because I'm sure she will help us, 'we have to return the stolen vase to China.'

But Mina gets our attention with a shake of her head, half-laughing, half-disappointed. 'It was a fake. Mum really did buy it from a two-dollar shop in the eighties,' she says.

Everybody laughs. Our adventure on the roof feels **scary** and **exciting** enough that I don't even mind.

Boring Lady pulls a huge red scarf from her handbag and passes it to Jessie. 'From now on,' she says, 'any time you guys want to contact me, hang this in your window. I promise to look up at least three times a day.'

Jessie and Vee say excited thank-yous,

and Alice tries to tell her she doesn't need to.

Mina turns to Dad. 'I can show you how to lock your iPad so it only accesses Skype,' she says to him, but winking at me. 'Then Squishy Taylor can call her Mama in private without getting into other kinds of trouble.'

I suddenly realise something. **'Where's Baby?'** I ask.

Dad and Alice turn to each other in horror.

'He was asleep,' Alice says at the same time Dad says, 'We forgot him.'

We all **bolt** for the stairs, with Alice and Dad leading the charge.

Our apartment door is wide open. Standing in the middle of the kitchen,

with Baby **giggling** and trying to
poke out his eyes, is
Mr Hinkenbushel.

The End

About the author and illustrator

Ailsa Wild is an acrobat, whip cracker and teaching artist who ran away from the circus to become a writer. She taught Squishy all her best bunk-bed tricks.

Ben Wood started drawing when he was Baby's age, and happily drew all over his mum and dad's walls! Since then, he has never stopped drawing. He has an identical twin and they used to play all kinds of pranks on their younger brother.